I0621852

MEGALODON
APEX PREDATOR

S.J. LARSSON

SEVERED PRESS
HOBART TASMANIA

MEGALODON: APEX PREDATOR

Copyright © 2016 by Severed Press

WWW.SEVEREDPRESS.COM

ISBN: 978-1-925597-12-7

PROLOGUE

The young boy stood on deck long after everyone had gone to sleep. He liked the rough seas and cold air of the Drake Passage. Even at the young age of ten, he was fascinated by experiencing actual exotic places in real life, and his father indulged his every whim.

The moon was near-full, stars bright and twinkling, and the boy could see the ocean lit up in magical silver and blue. He grasped the frigid handrails with bare hands and tried to see as far as he could into the night.

A slight, freezing breeze picked up, and the boy burrowed into his fur-lined leather jacket. On the wind, the boy could've sworn he smelled something like rotten fish parts. Specifically, the kind that already had bugs eating them, lying in the heat for days. But here, it was ice-cold.

Despite his thick coat, his arms brought a chill. He didn't like that wind and the smell it carried. This wasn't the ocean he knew. Then again, he had come here to experience a new sea. Right where the Pacific and Atlantic Oceans met, as far south on Earth as he could get. Maybe this was part of these waters, but the boy felt in his gut that smell wasn't supposed to be there, and it especially wasn't supposed to be so close and strong.

He wasn't allowed to be out of bed in the middle of the night, and suddenly, he was so frightened that because he'd disobeyed, he was now going to be punished in a most awful way. Waves kicked up around the yacht and the boy's tender stomach heaved. He puked right onto his hands, still grasping the icy handrail, as the boat shifted high and low in the now incredibly rough seas.

The boy heard yells, but when he tried to turn and run to the voices, his hands had frozen to the metal handrail. His vomit had

1

stuck them stiff to the bar in moments in the sub-temperature Antarctic night.

"Dada!" he cried out, but his own voice was squeaky and weak. Nobody could have heard him. He turned to the handrail again, hearing more people onboard calling out. The boy yanked as hard as he could on his hands, but they wouldn't budge. Panic gripped him hard as that god-awful smell hit him again, but this time, it was in a blast of warm air from seemingly nowhere.

The people on deck behind the boy silenced all at once, and he saw flashlights and torches turn in his direction. He started shaking all over, slowly, ever so slowly raising his head to see what the lights had fixed on.

The warm air blew again, bringing the dead scent. He stared right into the most enormous, gaping, pointed-toothed white mouth ever imagined by a boy in his most secret nightmares. Teeth so big they were the size of his arms. His whole body would fit four times over in that mouth…

He dropped his jaw and wailed, "Dada!" He yanked on his hands and freed three fingers, not caring a lick about the blood pouring out from under his grip.

The mouth came closer. It had seemed like it was right about to eat him, but the boy realized the beast was so huge that there was still distance between the boat and the creature. The mouth. The ever-so-sharp teeth. Its breath, so strong it made the icy air warm, and so putrid only death could be the beast's insides.

He screamed now.

Arms grabbed him from behind. "Got you, son, now let go!" It was his dad. His dad would save him.

"My hands! They're frozen to the rail!"

His dad wrapped his huge, gloved fingers around the boy's bleeding hands and pried them off with a quick rip. The boy didn't make a sound. His eyes stayed fixed on the beast bearing down on the boat from the water.

He let himself fall limp in his father's strong hands, one arm under the boy's tush and the other under his arms with his heavily beating heart pressed against his father's own. His father dashed them across the swaying, rocking deck to the far side, back of the boat, away from the lifeboats and other people. The boy didn't ask questions. His hands now ached and he peeked at them. The moonlight showed flesh torn from them in strips, and black blood soaked his palms and fingers. He'd left his father's coat arms discolored from tops to elbows.

"What is it, Dada?" the boy whispered into his father's ear.

"I don't know. I just don't know, but we have to get away from it."

As they stood at the edge of the water, the boy couldn't stand it, and looked over his father's shoulder. He had to see how close the teeth were because the smell was worse than ever, and a burst of screams had risen up from behind them.

Now the boy saw the side of the thing, and it had to be some kind of great white shark. But it couldn't be a great white. Great whites weren't that big! The boy had seen them before. This thing was at least twice the size of one of those. Its gaping mouth rose high into the air above the boat, and it was as though it had neck bones because it turned its massive white head down to the deck, and the boy swore its teeth popped out of its mouth as it demolished the ship easily into a million pieces.

The boy flew off into the night sky and into the rough, freezing water, but his dada didn't let go for an instant. His grip didn't loosen in the slightest.

The boy couldn't breathe once in the sea. He'd never felt cold like this, and it was as though he'd never be able to unclench his chest again to take another breath.

"Come on, son, we have to swim. We have to swim far and fast, so you climb on my back, wrap your arms under my armpits, and don't be afraid."

"I'm not afraid, Dada." His weak voice shook from the lie and the air finally leaking into his frozen body. His father shifted him to his back and he gripped his father under his arms as tightly as possible.

The boy had to look back. The screaming was too much. He'd met these people and sailed with them for a week now. They were dying, he wondered, weren't they? That giant thing was killing them, eating them.

Or they were drowning.

He hoped that's what it was.

His father swam and swam, but the boy kept smelling the rotted fish as his hands burned in the frigid salty sea. Was this happening? Could this be real? He had to look again.

The boat was in pieces. The boy saw people in the water, but no sign of the giant beast…until the boy noticed a long, pointed thin fin sticking out of the water. It was so huge that to the boy, it seemed like the creature was inches from him and his father, and he screamed without thought.

"Shh, now, son. Quiet." His father's voice was labored from the icy and frantic, desperate swim.

The boy kept looking over his father's shoulder. He simply couldn't take his eyes off that fin—and then the giant creature's head came out of the water again. This time, the boy got a complete eyeful from the light of the bright moon.

Its pitch-black, gleaming eyes had to have been the size of cars each, and its awful mouth never seemed to close. The giant shark bent its strange head again, but instead of devouring a ship, it chowed down, hard, on passengers from the boat in quick, stabbing chomps. The boy finally closed his eyes right as he saw Ms. Engle, her shirt ripped off, disappear into the beast's cavernous jaws, its head tilted up as though drinking her like a milkshake, and he heard her terrorized, pain-soaked but short-lived screams of horror as the giant thing chewed her to pieces in a few short bites.

"Hold tighter," the boy's father said. "There's a piece of the ship ahead. We have to get out of this freezing water, but keep quiet. I don't know what that thing is, but we cannot draw any, and I mean any, attention to us whatsoever. Do you understand me?"

The boy kept his eyes closed, wishing he could plug his ears from the wails of the others from the ship being eaten and gored. He nodded against his dad's neck.

It could have been hours or minutes, but the boy's father got them to a piece of debris, hauling the boy out of the water before pulling himself up next to his son.

"You can open your eyes now," he said softly.

The boy didn't.

"They're all gone, son. It's just you and me."

"And *it*?" His voice was as weak as a baby pup offering up its first whimper.

"It's gone. I promise. Open your eyes."

The boy opened one eye. The sea had settled, and there was more ship debris floating all around them. He closed his eye when he spied what looked like the captain's arm, still in its skipper jacket, floating a few feet away.

"Don't you realize what we have just seen?" his father whispered. A freezing wind answered him before he continued. "That—thing. It shouldn't be here. Did you see its skin?"

He opened his eyes. The boy shook with adrenaline, fear, cold, and pain in his hands, but his father didn't seem to notice. His eyes gleamed in the starlight settling over the freezing sea, and for a moment, the boy allowed his father's enthusiasm to sink into him. He had just seen the unbelievable. Yes, he had.

But he had also seen Ms. Engle get chewed up alive by eight-inch shark teeth in a mouth big enough for four people.

His father continued. "The Megalodon. They were giant sharks, dinosaurs. Some say they were as big as sixty feet long. That one, that one was about forty feet, wouldn't you say, son?"

The boy didn't want to stop his father's excitement, but his hands wouldn't stop bleeding. They had to find some way to land, away from the giant beast, the huge teeth, and the ungodly cold. "Dada," he started hesitantly. He could barely talk, he was so weak. So much blood lost.

His father's eyes stayed focused on the ship's wreckage as he murmured, "Megalodon. There's one alive, son, and we found it. Do you have any idea what this means?"

"Dada, my hands."

His father looked down at the boy's shredded palms. "Oh, son. Oh my god, son." He wrapped his wet arms around the boy and tucked his head under his chin, rubbing the tops of his son's arms. "I'll get you out of here. It's okay. It's okay. We'll get out of here, and then we'll tell the world what we've found here today. I know you're scared and cold, bleeding, but we made it. Now, we have to survive. We have no choice. We must tell the world a prehistoric creature is still alive down here. We have to—"

The boy smelled the rotten fish smell so strongly that he felt bile rise up in his throat again, and he pulled back from his father, peeking over his shoulder to the warm gust of air accompanying the foul stench.

Nothing but jagged, sharp teeth filled his vision. The giant shark was right on top of their little island of debris, their piece of momentary and illusionary safety. At this range, the boy noticed each tooth seemed to have jagged teeth of its own. Teeth with teeth.

Then the jaws did that thing again. They seemed to shoot out of the massive creature's head, but this time, the beast snapped the chunk of metal they had been floating on in half, leaving the boy alone on his side, and his father in the teeth of the beast.

His father didn't scream; instead, all the boy heard, because his eyes were shut so tightly he might never see again, was the crunching of his dada's bones, and harsh, heavy grunts and gasps coming from his father's body as the shark demolished him into pieces of meat.

The boy balled up with his bloody fists under him and his backbone pointed to the sky, fetal, wishing, hoping, praying that it would *just go away*.

And if it did, he swore, absolutely swore by the tears in his soul at having heard his father die such a base and terrorizing death, that he would make it to land, and he would make it his life's goal to do what his dada wanted in his last moments. His dada had wanted it so much he forgot to keep paddling them on the debris.

The boy would make the world know. He would find a way to make sure everybody on the planet knew this thing was here, right here, in the Drake Passage, if it was the last thing he did in his life.

CHAPTER 1

Will had always hated the cold, and now, after six months so close to Antarctica, his father had finally brought Will and his sister aboard his ship for the great Drake Passage expedition he'd been hired for and getting ready for, along with the dozen or so passengers from England.

Who would want to see this place?

Will hadn't gotten his sea legs, even at twelve. His dad blamed it on how he was six feet tall, and grew four of them in the past year.

He had to stay in open air to keep his stomach somewhat settled. Anytime he went into the stagnant, bottled-up warm air of the cabins, he eventually ended up swallowing puke until he made it back outside.

So, basically he had to stay in the most frigid outside place on the planet all the day, or stay warm and vomit in his mouth every few minutes.

He'd found the higher up he was, the less the lingering seasickness, even in the fresh air, bothered him. As he'd been doing whenever they were at sea, he now rested on top of the breezy bridge's roof with his legs crossed, and his hands and arms buried in the crooks of his knees. He kept his head down. There wasn't much to seeing the ocean after doing so for most of his life.

It was close to sunset, and Will caught a glimpse of movement below on deck. He lifted his head to see who it was.

Sir Jeffery Mallory stared right back up at him. In his smooth, strong voice, he called up to Will, "In your spot?"

Will loved Sir Mallory's English accent. He nodded.

"Come down. You'll freeze your nose off up there when it gets dark." He smiled a perfect white grin.

Will scrambled to get his stiff muscles moving and climb off the bridge roof to Sir Mallory. He'd been enchanted with the fifty-year-old rich Brit since the man gave him an English pound within moments of their meeting. That coin was cool. He kept it in his pants pocket all the time.

Once on deck, Will only slightly looked up to meet Sir Mallory's eyes, the older man having a couple inches on him. Sir Mallory clapped Will's shoulder and said, "Your dad is one amazing sailor. He's a natural. So pleased he agreed to my proposal because nobody can sail the Drake Passage like Captain Miller."

Will nodded. "He was even born on a boat."

Sir Mallory's laugh was thick, rich, and contagious.

Will grinned, bad mood dispelling. He didn't feel as cold.

Sir Mallory leaned in toward him and in a soft, joking tone, said, "You, on the other hand, were probably born on the hard, packed earth as far away from the ocean as possible."

Will looked down, but couldn't help but give off a small smile.

"Oh, don't be embarrassed. I'm a diabetic, have to take insulin shots. When I was a kid, I was mortified if anyone knew I was taking my shot. Silly things, insecurities." He looked at Will with one eye squinting against a cold wind picking up. "Funny thing, most people are so worried about their own insecurities that they don't realize everyone has them. You have them. I have them. Even bugs in the soil have them. It's survival."

"Do killers have them?" The bold question sprung from Will's mouth before he could think about how inappropriate it was.

Sir Mallory turned his head away from the wind and examined Will with a twinkle in his electric green eyes. "Killers have every insecurity."

Will grinned back at him. Sir Mallory didn't think twice about his odd question, and his reply gave Will something to think about. He loved how Sir Mallory treated him like an equal, didn't ask him about his studies in Argentina and what he liked to do in his spare time, like so many adults did when they had no clue he wasn't eight anymore.

Will also picked up that Sir Mallory had charmed the crew of his father's charter boat, and all of the people Sir Mallory brought along for the exploration often laughed and joked with him.

Will's father had told him and his sister that Sir Mallory knew the true meaning of catching more flies with honey.

"Want to see something you've never seen before? Touch it, hold it? Something that once belonged to a killer?" Sir Mallory's eyes kept sparkling, but now with mischief and daring.

"Yeah!" said Will.

Sir Mallory dramatically looked over both shoulders as though making sure nobody was watching, even though the rest of the shipmates hid below deck from the cold. Will giggled. Sir Mallory reached into the huge left pocket of his parka, and out came the biggest, sharpest tooth Will had ever seen.

"What is that?" It filled Sir Mallory's whole palm and then some. "How big is that? That *is* a tooth, right?" He couldn't hide the wonder in his voice, and longed to hold the massive thing.

Sir Mallory read his mind, holding the giant tooth out to him. "It's a little over six inches long. It's a shark tooth. A prehistoric shark tooth, a shark called a Megalodon. Ever heard of it?"

Will took off his gloves, and ran his fingers and palms all over the gray, pointy, and polished tooth. The very edges of the tooth had serrated spikes going down along the sides. That gave his imagination a small shiver. "No, but it's dead now, right?"

Sir Mallory glanced at the setting sun. Orange filled the sky to the west. "The Megalodons supposedly died off two million years ago. Now, Will, that's not too long ago, is it?"

"Sounds like forever." He turned the tooth this way and that, admiring the polish shining in the sunset.

"All we have of them are their teeth. Some fossil markings in soil. But like all sharks, they were held together by cartilage, which dissipated long ago. People who study them really can't say what they looked like or how big they actually were, but most agree they were as long as sixty feet. Can you imagine?"

He shook his head, looked up at Sir Mallory, and held out the giant tooth to him. "Cool, thanks."

Sir Mallory took the tooth and put it back in his pocket. "You're welcome. Have you tried Dramamine? For the seasickness?"

"I've tried everything, but what works is just throwing up. I can't go around throwing up every thirty minutes." He rolled his eyes at Sir Mallory, then grinned. "School starts up after this trip and I'll be so glad to be on land. We'll be going back to the States."

Sir Mallory gave him an inquisitive look. "I haven't seen you blow chunks."

Will let out half a laugh, but said nothing.

"What? Don't be embarrassed. I'm dying to know now."

Will shrugged. "It's gross, but I throw up in my mouth, then swallow it back down. I just don't eat or drink much when I'm on a boat, so there's not much that comes up."

His face dropped in sincere sympathy. "You poor guy. How miserable. They say everybody eventually gets their sea legs, but Will, I think you're the guy who never could ride a bike all his life."

That made Will laugh, and he appreciated that Sir Mallory made him feel less self-conscious about his inability to physically cope with the motion of the ocean.

CHAPTER 2

Will was bundled up with three space heaters blowing on him on the bridge. He spent nights on the bridge with open windows and the space heaters to keep from barfing while staying warm. Nights in this part of the world didn't leave room for even the sickest person to get fresh air outside.

The watch his dad gave him on his tenth birthday said it was seven at night, just past.

As if on cue, Ellen, his sixteen-year-old sister, entered with a hot plate of fish and vegetables. "Come on, Willie, you gotta eat something. Look, it's fresh-caught." She held the food under Will's nose, but his stomach turned. Still, he took the plate and offered her what he thought was a genuine smile.

"I'm not leaving until you have at least three bites. Big ones." She stood straight, chin-length brown hair falling over one eye, and put her hands on her hips with a frown.

Will picked up the tin fork and shoved the peas and carrots around. "I...I can't right now, but I will. You can leave it."

She huffed. "You're going to starve! You have to get some nutrients. Look. One bite, okay? Then I'll leave you to pick at it all night if you want to." She looked out of the bridge windows. "But you won't," she said in a sing-song voice.

"What do you mean?" His curiosity piqued.

"Well," she said as she crouched back down, "Sir Mallory is lighting the deck's fire pit tonight and is going to tell a story. Something about what this expedition is all about. I mean, Dad's been sailing the Drake Passage for months now getting his chops back for this, and who knows how much Sir Mallory really is paying him to do it. I mean, he's a knight, for Christ's sake! Can you imagine the kind of money he has?"

"Nobody ever told me what he was knighted for." The smell of the cooked fish turned his guts and he put the plate next to him on the floor.

"I dunno, but it must have been bravery. Don't you think he's handsome? I mean, for an older guy. I like older guys."

"Eh."

She slapped his arm. "What did I tell you? One bite. Then at eight, be on deck. Now, go on, eat up."

Will picked the plate back up and took a nibble of fish. It actually tasted delicious, and he took another small bite.

"Good, good. See? Not so bad." She smiled at him. "I know this is the rough part, but I have this feeling, ya know? Like we're gonna see stuff, do stuff like nothing we've ever done before. Sir Mallory gives you that feeling, doesn't he?"

Will nodded. Sir Mallory certainly made an impression on him, but not exactly the heartthrob kind he had on Ellen. Will guessed he could see the older guy's good looks, but he suspected it was the knighthood that really got Ellen excited.

In a low voice, so Don Mack couldn't hear, she said, "Caleb is coming to my room tonight. Don't you dare pick my lock, and if Dad tries to make you, pretend you can't. Got it? Willie?"

"Who's Caleb?"

She blushed again. "He's one of the guys with James. He's eighteen, so smart he graduated from college this year. He's so interesting. But tonight, it's special, okay? No lock-picking."

He nodded. Ellen had gone from swooning over Sir Mallory to sneaking an eighteen-year-old into her cabin in less than a minute. "Okay, will not disturb in any way."

Ellen left Will to pick at his fish and vegetables, huddled in blankets and trying to keep the food down. He hadn't realized how hungry he'd been.

Don Mack, his dad's first mate, was at the wheel in front of Will, and he turned. "Look at ya. Eating like a regular sailor, son. Maybe you're starting to get those sea legs after all."

Will smiled weakly as a bit of fish rose up in his throat with a shift of the sea. He swallowed it back down without expression.

"Hey, Don?" Will asked him.

"Yeah?" He kept his eyes on the dark sea. The ice in the water wasn't as bad in this area, but it could still sneak up unexpected. Don Mack was almost as good as his dad at cold sailing.

"Do you know why Sir Mallory was knighted?"

He shook his head. "Don't give a crap."

Will's eyes widened. "Why not?"

He shrugged, pushed his enormous hat back. "It's a bunch of rich people giving other rich people a reason to feel more important. 'You are better than everybody else because I'm better, too, and I say so. You are a knight!'" He said the last part in what Will imagined was the Queen of England's mimicked voice. Don slapped his thigh. "Get it?"

Will chuckled. "Yeah. But don't you think Sir Mallory might be a little different or something? I don't get the feeling he's stuck on himself or all high-and-mighty."

Don turned for a moment. His nose was bright red and bulbous, and a lock of black hair fell out of the front of his hat and over his forehead. "I don't know what to make of the guy. Except he's up to something, and we're about to find out what."

"We are?"

He laughed. "Didn't you even listen to your sister?"

"Oh. The fire pit at eight."

"Yeah, yeah. The fire pit at eight. I have to float this boat and can't go, so you have to tell me everything. This expedition's been in the works for four years, and your dad's only just agreed after three years of Mallory begging him. Wouldn't do it without him. Something's up."

"Dad didn't say anything."

"Nobody knows what the expedition is all about."

"Well, Dad said it was secret, but I thought that was just from me and Ellen."

Don shook his head and kept his gaze on the horizon, lazily fielding the ship's wheel. "Big part of the reason your dad wouldn't sign on for so long is because Mallory wouldn't tell him what it's all about upfront. Somehow, Mallory convinced him to go along with it, anyway."

Will thought for a minute. "Did Sir Mallory give Dad a bunch of money to make him say yes?"

Don laughed. "I'm sure as hell he did, but I don't think that's why your dad said yes."

Will rubbed his face and pushed his dinner away. "I'm so confused."

"Your dad's a sailor. You know that."

"So? Of course he is. He sails all the time. But why in this freezing bottom of the planet?"

"Maybe he's a curious man. Could be nostalgia. Captain Miller sailed the Drake Passage for the first six years of his sailing career. Or maybe Mallory used that British charm and eventually got to him. But just between me and you, I don't think your dad likes Mallory much."

"Really? Why not?"

Don wiped his red nose. "Your dad's a straight-shooter. Mallory's a chummy talker. Two types that don't usually walk off into the sunset as best friends…ever."

"Dad's so judgmental," Will said under his breath. He couldn't help it. Every time his dad brought him to sea, Will's seasickness grew in him resentment toward his father until they were grounded, and then it would vanish with the spinning of Will's head coming full stop.

"Hey, don't say that. Your dad's one of the good ones. I'd trust him with my life. Hell, doing this trip with him *is* trusting him with my life, but you know what? He knows the Drake Passage so well it's like trusting him with a shotgun in a mad dog's face."

"Huh?"

"He knows how to use a shotgun real good, too. You seen it? You think he's something with that whip he carries around all the time. He just switched to that when Ellie was born. Oh, and the Glock, man. He's a wicked one with the Glock."

"What Glock? Dad doesn't have any guns." He thought of his dad's skills with the black whip. One of his father's favorite things to do was sneak up behind him and ensnare him around the waist. It always gave him a mean jump, but he guessed that was his dad's way of hugging. Other times, he'd seen his dad use the whip to catch fish right out of the sea.

"Oh." Don straightened up and rubbed his nose again. "I must have been thinking of when we'd go out when your mom was still alive. He could shoot a shark thirty feet away right in the face with his handgun and kill it instantly."

"Dad? For real? No way." Will tried to imagine his lanky, tall old man as a gunslinger. It was hard to think of his quiet, somber father ever unloading a gun into any living thing. "What was he like?" Will said quietly.

"Your dad? Always knew what to say. Always knew what to do. Still does. He's just more careful."

"No, I mean before. Like, when you'd sail with him, before Mom." Will was afraid to ask. His mother was an off-limits topic around his dad, and Will had never thought to ask Don. Before Will sprouted up to being taller than Don, the old sailor treated him like a fragile doll. Probably because he was sick every sea voyage. It was amazing how some things had changed since he'd hit six feet. Now Don Mack cursed in front of him, and Will had been surprised during those long nights on the bridge how much Don rattled on about whatever thought came to his mind.

"Your mother was the best, you know it. Pretty as a movie star. Your dad used to be a hell raiser, Will. Always quiet, always thoughtful, but daring and adventurous. That's what your mom liked about him." Don wiped his nose again.

"He still does stupid things."

Don spun on him with bright black eyes. "Stupid! I'm betting this expedition pays for your and Ellen's college, and three new, fast cars for the lot of you. Maybe even a place on the beach in Virginia when you go back."

"Money's a dumb reason to risk the most dangerous seas there are," he mumbled.

"That's because you're twelve, and you don't have to feed your kids and put good clothes on their backs. Besides, it's more than money. Your dad loves a challenge at sea, and he's done the Drake Passage more times than any captain alive. It's like his warped paradise. He gets excitement, he gets to use his chops. Those things are important."

"Dad doesn't get excited about anything."

"Well, what the hell's got you pissing all over your dad like this?"

Will instantly felt guilt. He should have kept his mouth shut. "I just don't like being at sea."

"Oh, I get it. And he makes you go on trips. You have six years and then you never have to even take a shower again if you don't want to. Cut your dad a break is all I'm saying. He's had it rough. And between you and me, and I'd never say this except I nipped a touch of rum earlier, but he hasn't been right since she died. He loved adventure, sure, but she was the great adventure of his life. We can all only hope to have what your mom and dad had at some point in our lives, even if it is just for a day." He looked back at Will and smiled. "Eat more. Almost eight, and I see some of Mallory's people starting up the pit. You're in for a treat. Fresh air and a hot fire. Actually, just save your food and eat it on deck. I bet you'll actually finish a meal tonight with that setup."

CHAPTER 3

The warmth of the fire pit flaming orange and yellow soothed Will like a lullaby. Everyone onboard sat around it except for Don Mack, heavy coats open to the heat and cheeks flushed with fire in the icy air. Sir Mallory paced across from Will, making jokes quietly with his people, and one older woman in particular. She had dyed blonde hair cut short around her face, high cheekbones, and wrinkles that were downright dignified. Even in her parka, she looked frail, delicate. Will wondered at how this elegant lady, who had probably never known cold like this, nor been at sea so long, seemed as cool as a white Persian house cat while Will still couldn't finish his dinner.

"Eat." Will's father's voice came from behind where Will sat next to Ellen.

"I will in a sec." He didn't want his dad to get that stern tone, the one that said no questions asked. Maybe that tone of voice came from his days of shooting sharks dead with handguns.

"I told him," Ellen said, rubbing Will's arm. "You eat up, and he almost did, but I guess he was tricking me."

"No, I had to stop. I'll have more soon." He looked back over his shoulder at his father's standing form towering above. The light from the fire made his weathered skin contrast in hues, the lines of a long and complicated life almost flickering with studious movement across his features as he kept his dark eyes focused on the fire pit. Everyone said Will had his father's eyes, but other than color, Will couldn't see it. He couldn't see any of his physical likeness from his father other than his height, with his father notching doorframes at six-foot-six.

"You've lost weight," his father said.

"Not really. I've always been skinny."

"Too skinny."

Will shrugged and slowly took a bite of cold broccoli. His stomach was somewhat settled, but food was the enemy at sea. Still, he wished he could sleep by the fire pit every night.

He could feel his father's disapproval in his voice, thus the piece of broccoli. It should keep him from being dissatisfied with Will for the moment.

Finally, just as Will thought the pretense of nibble after nibble was going to make him puke all over his sister, Sir Mallory turned all around the group with his hands in the air in front of him, palms out.

"Thank you, thank you," he said in a strong voice. "I want to thank every one of you who has come on our expedition. This will be one of the great times of your lives, I guarantee. Only a few I brought with me know the true nature for my wanting to come here. James." He turned to a guy in his thirties near him. Because of his heavy clothing, all Will could make out of him was that he had thick lips that turned up in the corners and pale skin. "James is our tech specialist. Head of tech. Tech head. And we do have some tech work ahead of us. He has a couple people he brought with him."

James waved a gloved hand and in a thick British accent, said, "Happy to be here."

"Next, we have Nancy. Nancy? Where are you?" He turned to a woman calling out to him.

"Right where you left me." She had red curls coming out of her parka hood, falling all the way down to her waist. She must be warm as a Husky with all that hair, Will thought.

"Nancy is a marine biologist with a specialty I've been looking for and nerves of steel. Thank you for coming, Nancy," Sir Mallory said, and bowed to her. She laughed.

"And then, of course I've told my wife." He turned to the woman with the short, blonde hair Will had noticed him talking with earlier. "Kathrine," he said, "it's because of you that the last thing I said I'd ever do is about to take place. Well, if all goes according to plan." He gave Kathrine a squeeze on her shoulder. She smiled stiffly from the attention as everyone stared at her, and pulled the hood of her coat back over her head.

"You told them. Why didn't you tell me?" Will's father's deep voice carried across the group. Will groaned under his breath.

Sir Mallory stood straight as he addressed Will's father. "Captain Miller, I didn't think I'd ever talk you into it until we got here, until you felt this part of the ocean again. The air, the ice. I thought you'd have to get the Drake Passage back in your blood before you'd understand, before you'd agree."

"You mean go along with your plan, right?" Will's father countered. It was obvious to Will that everyone around the fire pit felt the tension between the two men.

Sir Mallory tilted his head to the side and glanced at James, then back to Will's dad. "No worries, Captain Miller. You can still say no, and you'll be paid for the time you have put into this. Tonight, you will find out exactly what I have planned, and you can decide if it's worth it."

"Is there risk?" Will's father asked.

"Isn't there risk right now?"

"I mean for my kids. Real risk."

"Sailing the Drake Passage for any reason is risk, in my mind—but I will admit that yes, there is risk, but we have taken every precaution," Sir Mallory said with a smile.

"Alright," Will's father said. "Tell me."

Sir Mallory began pacing again. "I will. But first, I want to tell all of you a story, one I've only told my wife, and her only once. This will be the second time in my life I've spoken of an event in my childhood that took place right here in the Drake Passage, and that event has led me to undertake a lifetime of planning and study to execute a dream. But I digress. I'll now tell you what happened so long ago when I was just ten years old." He stopped, looked at his wife, and then his gaze swept over the group, landing on Will. The knight's eyes twinkled at recognizing him, even though Will was buried in layers of clothing, as though he wanted Will to hear this story more than anyone aboard. It made Will feel special, that this trip might actually be something special like Ellen had said. Sir Mallory smiled at Will, a gentle curve of the lips, different from his usual sunshine grins.

"My father, Jonathan Mallory, was a great man. I was the luckiest kid alive to have him as a father. He wanted me to experience anything I wanted, and he had the money to make it happen. He came from old money, and our family at one time held a title, but that's in the history books. Yes," he said with a chuckle, "he spoiled me right rotten. When I was ten, I told my father that I wanted to see the ocean where the Pacific and Atlantic met. I wanted to sail the Drake Passage. He made it happen. He found someone who would take us as close to Antarctica as north of Elephant Island.

"Everything about the voyage there was exhilarating, and I was never happier than when I spent times like those with my father. I wish I could imbed in all your minds the man he was so you'd know, understand. You'd understand why this expedition is so important."

Will noticed everyone hung on Sir Mallory's words like they were coming from a levitating magician. He peeked over his shoulder at his father, whose face was expressionless, but Will sensed distrust in the way his father crossed his arms and refused to sit like the rest of them. Plus, he'd interrupted Sir Mallory when he'd had the spotlight, dampening the mood.

He turned his attention back to Sir Mallory, who now squatted close to the flames in the fire pit, putting on a couple more logs to brighten the fire. "It's the winds," he said. "The gales here." He looked up over Will's head to his father behind him. "Sailing the Antarctic currents and temperatures, and all that goes with it is one thing, but the winds here, they change. Every hour or so. We've all felt it, but the deeper in you go, the more…" His eyes strayed down to Will's own. "The more your body reacts to the motion those gales bring, those constant changes in your body leaking into your soul."

Will stared back at him, stomach completely still. He couldn't look away for anything.

He stood, now looking into the fire. He pushed the hood of his coat back. His cheekbones hollowed out a long, thoughtful face in the fire's light. "It happened one night. We were on a small boat. Maybe ten of us, my father and I included." He paced, looking at the cloudy, black sky. "That night we were attacked by a sea creature. It smashed the boat to bits in a second with its very teeth, so big it may as well have simply swallowed the whole little ship and us along with it in one go."

He looked around the group before continuing. "My father saved my life. He got me away from it, into the sea and onto a piece of metal from the boat that was floating in the freezing water. I saw and heard my shipmates die at its bloodthirsty whims. And then, just when I believed we were going to be alright, when it was gone and the water had steadied, I smelled it. Oh yes, it has a very distinctive scent. It took my father from me then."

He put his head down and rubbed his closed eyelids. Nancy stood up and touched his elbow, whispering if he was okay.

He nodded to her, patted her shoulder. "Thanks. Hard to talk about." He looked around the group and began his pacing as Nancy sat back down. "The captain had called in for help already, and the creature left me alone for reasons I know not. Maybe I was too small to have a scent, but I was bleeding. I simply don't know. After several hours, I was rescued.

"When asked what happened, I told no one. I didn't think they'd believe me, and I was too horrified by it to speak of it yet.

"When pushed, I realized I had to say something, so I told everyone there had been a terrible storm." He stopped pacing and stood in front of the fire pit, staring into it, his cheeks getting color back into them. "Captain Miller," he said, looking up at Will's dad. "Do you know of this creature?"

Will's father put his hand on Will's shoulder, but said nothing. He glanced at his sister, and his father's other hand grasped her shoulder, too.

"My father called it a Megalodon, and after all my studies, I believe a Megalodon, the two-million-year extinct prehistoric giant shark, the apex predator, lives in the Drake Passage north of Elephant Island." He kept his steady and intense gaze on Will's dad. "They are not extinct; or, at least, one isn't."

Will's father squeezed Will too hard as he said, "What exactly do you have in mind for us here, Mallory?" His voice was low, and rumbled with anger.

A low, tight breeze kicked in hard, and Will pulled his parka around him, ducking his head instinctively to block his eyes from drying out in the gust of wind. He didn't get to see Sir Mallory's expression, and his dad's grip didn't loosen.

Will shielded his face and eyes, and squinted up at Sir Mallory as the man called out over the sound of the wind, "I want to catch one." His jaw set as he challenged Will's father with his eyes, green and flashing in the brighter-than-ever firelight.

Will's father pulled both him and Ellen to their feet in a sweeping movement by the scruffs of their coats. "Are you fucking mad?" he yelled over the wind, which had blown his hood off. His thin, brown-and-gray hair spun like cotton pulled every which way.

"Dad? What the hell?" Ellen said, yanking away from him.

Will tried to twist out of his grasp, but his father squeezed hard on his upper arm and spun him to face him. "You." He looked at Ellen. "You take him, and you go to the bridge. We're turning this ship around."

"Captain Miller," Sir Mallory yelled. "You have seen one. You know about the Megalodon here. You do!"

"What are you freaking out over, Dad? Are you okay?" Ellen said, hiding her face from the stinging breeze.

"Dad," Will said, but his father ignored him and told Ellen again to take Will to the bridge. "Dad!" he called out, making sure to be heard. "Dad!"

Slowly, his father turned and looked down at him with worry etched in his face. "What?"

Will blinked. "Is it really a Megalodon? A giant shark?" He squinted as the wind changed direction. "Have you seen one?"

His father's eyes saddened, and then went firm with resolve. "No, you two go now. That's it. That's all." He pushed them toward the bridge, where Don Mack would be waiting to hear everything.

"We better go. I've never seen him like this," Ellen said to him, pulling him along.

He glanced back, hearing Sir Mallory beg his father to at least speak in private with him before being so completely set against it. He had plans; he had somewhere nearby already built to take it…and then Will was out of earshot.

Ellen filled Don Mack in on everything that happened once they were on the bridge. Will's stomach churned with the motion of the ship from the strong gales. He sat huddled in blankets on a chair, hanging his head out a side window, skin stinging, looking out at the black water churning around them. Once in a while, he heard raised voices.

He felt conflicted. Sir Mallory's story was outrageous, but Will believed something happened. The man couldn't have been more sincere as he told his story. His father's reaction told Will that he knew something about it. Like, his father actually had seen the same sea creature at some point when he sailed down here way back when his carried a Glock.

As he closed his eyes to the shifting wind, anger brushed up inside him. His dad brought them all the way down to South America for months, and now to the deep Antarctic sea, and was going to turn around without explaining himself to Will? No, that wasn't going to happen.

Will wasn't one to stand up to his father about anything at all, but right then he thought he could have punched his dad in anticipation of the conversation they were going to have as soon as Will laid eyes on him again. For Will, there was no turning back.

Why? Because Sir Mallory was right. This would be one of the great adventures of his life, and he'd had so few. Sure, they might go hunting for the creature for a week and come home with nothing, but what if they didn't? Sir Mallory would have to be pretty sure about where to go and what to do in this whole situation to finally bring it to fruition.

Will wasn't going to let anything mess that up. Certainly not his father being overprotective.

True, in the end, his father had the yay-or-nay say, but Will had to know why, and it had to be the truth. And it had to defeat any reasoning Will could throw at it.

He opened his eyes and let them sting, tears from the wind blowing across his freezing cheeks. He didn't look forward to a confrontation with his father, but he had to do it.

He thought of the huge tooth Sir Mallory had let him handle. The Megalodon tooth. Those spiked edges. How big would the giant shark be? Will couldn't imagine catching one. Sir Mallory must have airtight plans, that was for sure. A giant shark was, indeed, a great killer. To catch one would change Will's life forever.

His father was going to use the tone on him, try to shut him down, but he wasn't going to let him. Will was fighting for this with everything he had.

He also knew deep down that if anyone could change his father's mind, it was him.

CHAPTER 4

"You will not question me," Will's father said quietly.

When he'd joined Ellen, Don Mack, and Will on the bridge, Will's boiling point had been reached and he'd snapped. He'd yelled at his father, saying things he never thought could come out of his mouth directed at the man. Ellen had been stunned, and Don Mack simply kept steering, eyes forward.

Will's dad told Don and Ellen to leave him alone with his son and took the wheel, back to Will.

"I will question you! You have to tell me why you won't do this. What is it? Have you seen things? A giant sea creature? You had forty years before Ellen was born. What did you do during all that time?"

"Now's not the time or place. I know best, and it's not safe for you or Ellen, what Mallory proposed." His dark eyes hardened and he kept his arms steady, standing tall.

Will stood up from his window. He felt tears threatening from the confrontation, fear and the intensity of speaking his angry mind to his father in his enraged state. "It could be the greatest thing any of us have done!" He glared up at his father.

He shook his head, looking down. "You don't know what you're talking about."

"But you do. Why'd you bring us here, then? If you knew something might be out here, I mean."

"I had no idea of Mallory's true plans. They are ridiculous. Even if there were a giant sea creature, even a Megalodon, of all things, do you really think we'd stand a chance against it?"

"Sir Mallory said he had plans. They brought all that secret cargo onboard. They know what they're doing."

His father paused and his expression lightened a bit. "We don't have the slightest clue what they have planned. All we heard was a man's dream for a hunt and nothing to back up how it would be done."

Will was not charmed by his father's relaxed expression. His voice got rough as he said, "You didn't even let him explain it. He offered to talk to you in private, tell everything, but no. You had to be hardheaded."

His face got stern again. "I'm not risking two children, my children's lives for this far-fetched fairytale. And if it is true, it's too dangerous. So many things can go wrong. Will, I'm sorry. I like seeing you interested in something at sea, but this isn't the way to go."

Will pushed his hands down his face. Anger and reason weren't working.

"When you're older, you can make these decisions on your own. But you're twelve. It's my job to make these kinds of decisions for you."

Will looked up at him. "If we weren't aboard, would you do it?"

His father hesitated.

"Would you at least have heard Sir Mallory out? Before saying no?" Will prodded.

He shrugged, eyeing Will carefully. "It doesn't matter. That's not what's happening."

Will's father wasn't the affectionate type, but despite, Will walked over to him and grasped his shoulders in his gloved hands, turned him to face him. "Dad, I want to do this. I want this experience. Look at you. You've been through it all, seen things most people never even know exist." He lowered his voice as his father met his eyes, unblinking, worried. "I want to do it. Dad. I'm old enough, strong enough. Nothing might happen. But something could. Please, for me, think. I need this."

He let his hands slip from his father's arms upon realizing his dad's expression wasn't changing. He turned and went back to his window. Without looking back at his father, he said, "You deserve to let me have this. Just this one thing. Of all the boats you dragged me on, all the moves for jobs, you never being there half the time, you owe me. And I'm old enough. I can take care of myself."

He let the cold wind sting his nose and cheeks. His father must have gone because it was quiet for a long while. Will didn't look behind him. It was so unfair. He'd finally spoken to his father as an equal, stood up for something, and the man ignored him and walked out without a word.

Suddenly, his father spoke. Will bonked his head on the top of the window frame in surprise at his baritone, soft and cracking. "You're right."

Will turned to him, away from the window. He had his arms at his sides, head cocked at Will.

"What do you mean, I'm right?"

"I'll make a compromise with you. I'll have that one-on-one talk with Mallory after I leave you. And I want you to sleep."

"What are you going to ask him?"

His father rubbed his face. "I'm going to find out all the details of his plan. If I think it sounds like it will work, or couldn't work, I will reconsider and make my decision."

Will hopped up, standing a few feet from his father, eyes lit up with excitement. "For real? You mean it? But what changed your mind?"

He smiled at Will, the corners of his eyes cracking in weathered wrinkles. Quietly, he said, "When I was your age, Will, I lived on my own. I never told you that. That's how I got into sailing. A crew took me on for work. I was twelve, just like you, and I could handle it. I suppose you can, too. But not until I hear all the plans Mallory has."

"I just know he's got this," Will said, showing his trust in the knight.

His father's face darkened a moment, and then he leaned down toward Will's face, cupping him behind his neck. "I'm on your side. Remember that."

CHAPTER 5

Sir Mallory certainly must have had everything planned to a T.

They arrived north of Elephant Island the next afternoon. Will hadn't been able to sleep while his father sailed them just out of reach of Antarctica through ice, wind, and wild currents throughout the night.

He'd been with Sir Mallory for three and a half hours after leaving Will on the bridge the night before, Don Mack taking over for the time being, according to Will's watch. He had been nervous, which had made his nausea worse, but when his dad finally came on the bridge afterward, relieved Don Mack of duty, and took the wheel, Will couldn't help but at least utter, "Oh, yeah!"

His father then looked back at him. He smiled and wiggled his eyebrows, a glimpse of adventure in his eyes. Not something Will saw much of, and he liked it. That was that.

Will had been dying to hear details of the plans, but knew better than to pry. He'd said enough that night.

He went out on deck to feel how cold it was down there in the cloudy daylight air. He'd never been so far south. Surprisingly, a lot of people were out and about. A light snow fell, but they were fat flakes that blew away with the breezes.

Sir Mallory stood by a rail, looking into the sea below. Will walked up to him, thinking maybe he could ask a few questions about the plan. Drop leading hints, at least.

"Hi, Sir Mallory," he said, now standing by his side. He looked down into the water in case Sir Mallory saw something cool, but Will saw nothing.

"Oh," Sir Mallory said, head cocked at him with a smile. "You're a ninja, of course you are. Didn't hear you come up on me."

He felt shy suddenly, not knowing what to say, but then Sir Mallory turned to him, elbow on the rail, and looked into his eyes. "You changed your father's mind."

Will's eyes widened, but he said nothing.

"Your father respects you, and that is a great thing for a child to have from his parent." He laughed softly. "What I'm curious about is, what made *you* want to do this?"

Will looked down a moment, but decided to be as short and honest as he could. "I want to try. I think you know what you're doing, too."

He chuckled, looking down. "I think you'll like the facilities on Elephant Island. That is where I built the enclosure, and beyond is a compound with every comfort. There is a satellite feed."

"Wow." They both looked out over the snow flurries tapping the rough sea.

Finally, Will asked, "How are you going to find it? The Megalodon?"

"Well, as you might have noticed, I was a bit distracted when you approached. Sharks can detect small amounts of blood in water from miles away. This is the exact area I was attacked so long ago. This knife," he said as he pulled a switchblade from behind his right hand, "was poised to slice my arm and spill blood into the water when you walked over. It's sure to draw the sharks in the area, including the Megalodon. I'll do it every day until we must leave."

Will stared at the shiny silver blade. "Are you going to do it now?"

"I was going to, but I'd rather talk to you until you're bored with me, and then I'll do my part."

Will eyed him. "I want to see."

Sir Mallory raised an eyebrow to him, and then rolled up the many sleeves on his left arm. In a quick slash, he made an inch gash across his forearm and bent over the rail, squeezing his own blood into the Antarctic sea below.

Will winced, hiding it from Sir Mallory. It had to hurt, but the man made no expression.

Sir Mallory wrapped a piece of linen around the wound and tucked his arm back into volumes of clothes. "Now we wait."

"Dad didn't tell me, but what happens if...one comes?" He couldn't get more hint-laden than that.

He grinned broadly. "I'm going to put it into a deep sedation, tow it to my enclosure built just for it, and show the world over satellite what exists here in the Drake Passage. Simple as that. If you believe in such a thing, I think one could say it's written that way in the stars."

Will grinned.

"Now, the blood's done, I have to get some of my men ready in case it shows. It comes fast, but we're faster and we have sonar, equipment. Top-of-the-line. Will, you keep an eye out, too. You have a keen sense of observation." He smiled once more and walked away toward some of his people.

Was he observant? Nobody had ever said that to him. Quiet, yes, but he felt like he missed so many subtleties in the way people interacted.

Will's stomach was getting the better of him, so he climbed on top of the bridge and wished the sun was out. He watched the people on deck and realized all of them were Sir Mallory's men. None of his dad's crew was outside.

They opened the secret boxes the English group had brought aboard, but inside, everything was either wrapped up, or Will couldn't make out what in the heck the objects were. They left one large steel case untouched.

James, the tech guy, on the other hand, had all kinds of gadgets and computer stuff set up, including some kind of oscillating dish. He sat with it surrounding him in a circle in the center of the deck near the fire pit.

Nancy, of the long red ringlets, dealt with several medium-sized freezers, with younger girls helping her. Will tried to see what was inside of them each time she opened one to do whatever she was doing with them, but no luck.

The most mysterious of all, though, were the four guys, big, strong, unassuming, who stood off by themselves by a rail drinking coffee. They all dressed in padded green suits under their winter garb. Will had seen them when they boarded. Who were they, and what part did they play?

Just then, Ellen grabbed his arm and got in his face. He hadn't heard her climb up. "Lady Katherine is all alone down there. Come on, Willie, let's go talk to her. Maybe she'll tell us why Sir Mallory was knighted." She giggled, blushing.

"No way."

"Oh, come on! I can't go by myself! Plus, she won't be rude to children. Please?"

He glanced at the elegant woman perched on a deck chair, shrouded in layers and coats. She read a book and her face was expressionless.

"Okay, I won't make you eat tonight, and I'll even throw the food out myself. Please?" Her big brown eyes begged.

"Oh, okay. Let's go."

They climbed down and approached Lady Katherine, who didn't take notice of them until they stood a foot away from her. She looked up quickly. "Oh, hello."

"Hi," Ellen said with a quiver in her voice. "I'm Ellen, and this is my brother, Will. We wanted to meet you." She smiled.

Katherine returned the gesture, but her lips seemed pinched, used to smiling when it was polite or for cameras. "Very nice to meet you. You're Captain Miller's children, correct?"

"Yes, ma'am," Ellen said, beaming.

Katherine closed her book. "And I suppose you have a question or two for me?" Her voice was smooth as silk, as cool as the flurries floating around them.

"Well, yes, actually," Ellen continued. "We're dying to know how Sir Mallory became knighted."

She gave Ellen a half-smile, eyed Will carefully, and then said, "An assassin was hired to kill me. Jeffrey and I didn't know each other at the time, but at a social gathering, the assassin took a shot at me. Jeffrey jumped in front of the bullet, saving my life."

"And he got knighted for that?" Ellen blurted out.

"Well," chuckled Katherine. "I have a direct bloodline to the queen. To save me ensured the queen's highest gratitude. And he was knighted."

"You didn't know each other, but fell in love and got married after?" Ellen sighed. "That's so romantic."

"Hmmm," Katherine hummed, opened her book and seemed to dismiss them.

Ellen looked at Will and shrugged. They walked away, and Ellen followed him to the roof of the bridge.

"It's weird how Dad just changed his mind," Ellen said once they'd settled in some blankets. She looked at him, but he was too embarrassed to meet her gaze. "I can't believe you yelled at him like that." Her voice, softer than the snow. "But you got through to him, and now...what happened after I left last night?"

Will finally looked at her. "I told him I wanted to. That I was ready."

Ellen shook her head. "Dad's ready, too. He loves this stuff, the rough seas, the challenges. You know what? I think when he saw it in you yesterday, it brought back something for him, something old and forgotten."

"Like what?"

She pushed her brows together and leaned her head to one side. "He's been smiling today. With his eyes, though, like he used to." She looked at him. "He never worries about me. I'm just like Mom. Level-headed and open-hearted. Pretty simple way to live, Dad told me once, and that it was glorious. He used that word."

"He's never talked to me like that."

"I bet he did last night. Did he?"

Will slowly nodded. "Yeah, he did. He listened. It was cool."

"And now, we're going to catch a prehistoric shark. How exciting is that?"

He grinned. "I hope we do."

"Oh, me too. It would be incredible."

They laughed too hard, one of those laughs that should have simply been a twitter, but evolved into gooning. They were breathing so hard that when the smell hit, Will's heavy breathing picked it up right away. It was as though he had let fly the fish from the night before and stuck his face in it.

"God, what is that?" Ellen said, covering her nose, laughter forgotten.

Will wrapped his scarf up around his mouth and nose, scanning the air around them.

Then, he looked at the deck.

People ran everywhere. James and his people's machines seemed to be in overload, with the dish spinning wildly. Nancy and friends dragged something enormous and clear into the water beside the ship, and then pulled the whatever-they-weres out of the freezers and threw them in the same place.

Sir Mallory and the four unidentified men carried giant fishing spears, all aiming south, where the wind blew the foul stench from.

The sea became restless while the snow swirled thickly. Ellen grabbed ahold of Will to keep her balance. Will tried yet again not to vomit on his sister, but it was from both the motion and the dead, rotting fish smell coming from everywhere.

He peeked over Ellen's bent head to the south of the ship and gasped at what he saw. The very sea itself seemed to be rising, rising in a tunnel, flanked by waves, enormous. Rough ocean splashed around the central rushing funnel, and then Will saw it—a gigantic, white dorsal fin, one that could only belong to a shark of unbelievable size, coming out of the water behind the rushing sea. It stood so tall, so very high and tall, that Will grabbed his sister's hand and with her, jumped off the roof of the bridge into the chaos of the deck.

CHAPTER 6

Instinctively, Will dragged Ellen to just behind Sir Mallory and the green-suited men, and most importantly, their spears. Will hoped desperately that the sedative Sir Mallory spoke of was in those—all of them. Because whatever was coming right here, right now in the late afternoon wasn't slowing down, and the closer the disturbance in the water, and the nearer the fin came, he felt a shock of fear that whatever sedatives Sir Mallory had picked for this…this…this whatever it was might not be right, couldn't possibly be strong enough.

The size of it. It was far away still, wasn't it? Was it so big that distance was distorted?

Time was definitely distorted, moving both at high-speed and in slow motion at the same time.

One of the men beside Sir Mallory called out, "Steady, steady. We need it closer!"

They all braced themselves.

The thing came closer at an unbelievable speed. Ellen squeezed Will's hand so hard his knuckles hurt.

The ship rocked to the side, away from the water rushing at it, from the fin and what it belonged to. The very force this creature's size plowed on the water was almost capsizing the boat before it even reached them.

Every piece of tech gear went over.

Everyone called out commands. Will crouched down with Ellen, arm around her. She stared up with him at the sky, right where the sea and fin had been. They leaned forward, hard, trying not to slide on the wooden deck.

The green-suited men and Sir Mallory were in front of them on their knees, and one of the men yelled, "We can't see her, we can't shoot her!"

"Captain Miller will fix this!" was Sir Mallory's reply.

It was Don Mack's turn at the wheel, not his dad's. Will glanced at the bridge windows.

Yes, Don Mack was there, but behind his father, who had somehow gotten there in time to…what? What could he possibly do?

Will's attention snapped back to the sky in front as the ship came back toward the sea monster and its gigantic fin. The ship tottered down, but stayed somewhat tilted. Will couldn't see the ocean, but yes, he could certainly see the long, thin white fin rising higher than Mt. Everest.

Will looked back at his dad, who had his focus completely on the horizon, not a thought seemingly on the fin.

And then Ellen screamed.

Will whipped his head around to see what freaked her out. Ellen wasn't the screaming type. His jaw dropped when he saw, but no sound came out.

An absolutely giant mouth full of row upon row of eight-inch teeth bore down on their tilted ship, coming down right on the deck where they all were. A small house could fit in that mouth, Will thought weakly, and then had no other thoughts. He was blank with confusion and disbelief.

"Fire!" Sir Mallory bellowed, and all five of them shot their enormous fishing spears into the oncoming tooth-filled maw.

They all landed, one hitting the tippy-top of the pointed white nose that showed above the mouth.

The mouth closed instantly, taking the million teeth with it, but the boat kept tilting, the creature's approach not slowed in the least.

Will's dad did something, and the boat flipped to where Will saw sky again just as the giant shark slammed its face into them. The entire ship skidded like a skipping stone across the icy water's surface and came to a slow slippery slide at what felt like two hundred yards away from where they'd been hit.

The boat righted almost immediately upon its momentum slowing.

Will puked all over his coat.

Will's father's voice came from the coms. He told his crew to reinforce the hull, check the ship for damage, fix, fix, fix. But he stayed at the wheel, now eying the horizon where they'd been moments ago.

Will looked, too, and stood, helping Ellen up.

He could see the thing now. He figured it all out now.

Nancy and her girls had been throwing in some kind of net with food for the Megalodon. The shark had been ensnared before it had hit them, or perhaps when. Sir Mallory and the green-suited men had shot sedatives, but what kind?

The thing had to be forty, forty-five feet long. It was shining, pure snow white, from the tip of its bleeding and stuck nose to its flopping tail splayed sideways in the water. Only its gills stood out, blood red and fluctuating madly.

What had they used on it? And was it enough? It wasn't sedated like you'd put down an elephant, asleep, but he guessed that might be hard to do with a fish. He wasn't even sure if sharks slept. This thing writhed and yanked around slightly, but stayed in place.

The boat was mostly steady, and his father turned them toward the giant shark, still twisting and twitching in the water.

Will's gut said, *stay away, go back and forget this. This was a bad, bad idea.* But, his heart pumped with adrenaline, and he felt a little smile on his lips, eyes wide. He wanted to see what happened next, absolutely had to, no doubt.

Right there, in front of him, was a Megalodon. And he was a part of the team who caught it.

When they got about twenty feet from the enormous beast floating in Nancy's clear net, Sir Mallory and his men shot it again, but this time with some kinds of handguns with darts. They aimed for those bright red gills.

The Megalodon turned upright and swam in place in its enormous clear net, almost as though awaiting instructions from its human gods.

"Thought it'd be bigger," a green-suited man said.

Sir Mallory nodded. "Me too."

"Still twice as big as a great white," Don Mack said from behind them. He'd joined soundlessly, and Will smiled at him.

"Did you see it?" Will asked him.

"I sure as shit did. And I sure as shit was glad when your dad took over, 'cause he saved us all."

Sir Mallory turned to Will as Nancy and her girls maneuvered the seemingly hypnotized gigantic shark to the back of the boat. "He's the only man alive who could sail against one, and you're the only man alive who could bring that desire out in him. See?" He smiled. "We all play our parts."

Will smiled back. "How are you getting it to act like that? It's like a robot. I'm not even scared of it when it's like this. I mean," he said quickly, knowing Sir Mallory would see right through his bravado, "I was terrified before, and it's still freaky, and I'm worried it'll change to bad again, but what did you give it?"

"I consulted Nancy on it, and my theory proved correct on great white sharks. First, a paralyzing agent. That was in the fishing spears. Not enough to stop the heart or needed functions, but the right amount to immobilize it." He leaned in. "This next part was my idea. It's called zombie dust, but the chemical is tetrodotoxin. Do you know what that is?"

"No." He shook his head, mesmerized.

"In Haiti, they make a dust out of it that they blow into people's faces. It makes them zombie-like, obedient. I used this in the darts. Look." He turned and pointed at the Megalodon, now attached to the back of the ship, looming out behind them for what seemed like miles. Peaceful. Just under the water. Enormous white fins swishing, a tail the size of their boat moving softly. Tall dorsal fin just showing a tip at the surface. A pup along for a walk. "We have to monitor it, but we have it. And now we'll take it to the compound. We'll be there before midnight."

CHAPTER 7

The weather in the Drake Passage was unpredictable at best, unforgiving the rest of the time. Within an hour of capturing the Megalodon, the flurries hardened into hail, with an easterly wind so forceful that walking on the hail in the gales kept everybody inside.

It drove Will mad, and he felt so damn sick huddled on the bridge with only cracked windows. He just wanted to watch the Megalodon. That's all. That's it. But no, this horrible place had other plans.

Day faded to night and the weather got worse. His father hadn't slept in two days. He had to do this sailing. Nobody else could, not even Don Mack. Not even for a moment. It was going to take a couple more hours to get to the Elephant Island compound in this weather, his dad said.

Will knew he'd stay up the whole night. Nothing could make him even think about drifting off, his adrenaline was so pumped.

His dad didn't talk much as he sailed, and Will had little to say. He'd gotten a fresh coat, but it was a little small on him.

The sea was awfully rough, and he was afraid that even though he'd only eaten breakfast, he'd barf bile if he opened his mouth.

Time passed this way, and Will kept thinking about that Megalodon they tugged behind them. Sir Mallory had said they grew to be sixty feet, but this one was smaller. What if it wasn't a Megalodon, but some other Antarctic giant shark they'd found? As far as Will knew, some bottom feeder sharks were huge, but nothing like the thing they'd caught that day.

Had his father really known what to do earlier, or had it been instinct? Had he gone up against this thing before? Will was dying to know, but didn't ask. Not only was he afraid to open his mouth out of fear of projectile vomiting, but the time wasn't right. His father was deep in concentration with no sleep. Will would ask once they'd rested at Sir Mallory's compound.

The evening passed that way, quiet except for the wind and the sound of hail hitting the ship. It never slacked off for a second.

Will looked at his watch around midnight, knowing it was frigid outside, but also knowing if he didn't get into some fresh air soon, his stomach would spill out and he would heave until he passed out from exhaustion.

"Dad," he said, his breathing labored. "I gotta go outside, just for a sec. Just for some air."

He glanced back at him. "Stay wrapped in blankets and no longer than ten minutes or you'll freeze."

"Yes, sir."

He dashed to the door, and even though the hail pelted him and the gales stung every inch of his face, he felt relief.

He stumbled down the bridge stairwell and to the deck, hanging his head over a railing, willing it to come, to get over with. And, finally, it did, and he retched into the Drake Passage stomach acid and water, then nothing at all over and over until he could breathe again.

Will took huge gulps of the freezing air, head pointed at the hailing sky, trying to get his head to stop spinning.

"Hey, you okay?"

He slowly turned to see Nancy, a few red curls coming out of a thick hood revealing who she was. "Yeah, just seasick. Alright now."

"Aw, you poor guy. Take anything for it?"

"There's nothing."

She patted his arm. "What a shame. Don't worry, we'll be at land in no time."

Will appreciated her comfort. "What are you doing out in this weather, anyway?"

"I'm watching the Megalodon. Came to get food. I have a tent set up in back, plenty warm. I don't suppose…" She smiled at him and jerked her head toward the back of the boat.

"You mean…actually go sit in the tent and…I can, like, watch it? I mean, it's too dark, right?"

"We have spotlights on its head. We take every precaution. Have to be sure the sedatives keep working."

The zombie dust.

"How much of that stuff do you have?"

She laughed. "Enough to take down twenty of them! Now, come on, and don't slip."

He thought about running and telling his father so he wouldn't worry, but excitement got the better of his judgment. He followed Nancy to the back of the boat where, indeed, there was a very warm-looking tent. One whole side was clear glass facing out on the head of the netted and obedient Megalodon, lit up by four spotlights. Will could only see the front of the ship from the bridge and had no idea all this was happening back here.

The tent was a little too warm, so Will dropped the blankets and took off his parka. He couldn't take his eyes off the Megalodon's face. It was wider than the ship, yet high cheekbones rose on either side of its predatory face. Its nose was pointed and had a pinprick dot from where the spear had landed earlier. Its eyes, so very pitch black and glossy, blank, empty of thought. Could a monster like this have thought, or was it the zombie dust? Were they all tricked by the drug's potency and this enormous shark could snap out of it anytime, eating the ship and everyone onboard?

No, Will didn't think so. He felt safe. After puking and dry heaving, he felt better than he had in a week. He decided to let himself revel in simply looking at it, as much as he could see, which was just past the red gills slowly breathing in and out. It was incredible to behold. This was his time, his moment. Nancy, beside him, stared as well. She had her own moment to celebrate. He wished for a small second that Ellen were there.

Will imagined Sir Mallory's moment would be when he used his compound's satellites and showed the world.

What moment of all this did his father cherish? Will couldn't imagine.

He decided to stop thinking and just watch. The shark was mesmerizing in its stupor. If Will hadn't seen those rows of teeth ready to devour all of them earlier that day, he'd almost find it peaceful. Just a fish in an aquarium. A sea-sized aquarium. It made Will wonder how big Sir Mallory's enclosure was.

Time passed. Will forgot all about worrying his father and felt content, even though the hail pelted the tent and the wind made the cold-proof fabric around them shake and sway.

The seas got rough again after a while, and Will's stomach turned. He didn't want to leave; he wasn't finished watching the Megalodon. But, he knew that inside this warm tent with those choppy seas, it wouldn't be long before another dry-heave spell hit him.

"Thanks, Nancy, for showing me. I better be going now," he told her with a weak smile. Just talking was hard.

"Of course. We have a big night soon. You'll see more, and I know neither of us will be sleeping."

She had no idea how true that would be.

Will left the tent after covering back up, and slowly made his way across the ship to the bridge. Halfway there, he retched overboard a few times. After, he wiped his chin and looked out over the black night and sea. He could see ice floating in the water. How did his dad sail in this?

His dad. Oh, man. He was going to be pissed. Maybe if Will explained…

Then the smell hit. That awful smell, the one he'd smelled earlier. He'd only smelled it that one time in his life, when the Megalodon first came.

Had it awakened from its sedated state?

Will looked back at the lights on the Megalodon in the net. No movement. He gagged again from the smell. No, it was coming from the same direction he'd just puked, out at sea.

The rough water became even more turbulent. Will grabbed the rail of the ship to steady himself. He squinted into the darkness, plugging his nose and breathing through his mouth, with one hand in a death clasp on the handrail.

The ice chunks floating in the distance were rising…higher and higher. Something was coming. And that something was another one of those…of the Megalodons. There was more than one in these waters, and now it made sense that Sir Mallory captured one on his first try. What if there were dozens, hundreds of them?

Will used every bit of willpower to detach himself from the rail and run to the bridge to warn his dad, and by the time he got there, the ship was tilted at such an angle that he had to climb the stairs on his hands and knees.

His father had the wheel in a death-grip, and barked at him, "Goddamn it, son, where the fuck have you been? We got another one. Now, get the hell down and stay here. No arguing, no backtalk. Get down!"

The rage and fear coming off his dad filled the air so much so that disobedience was not an option. He got in a corner and pulled his knees up to his chin. "Where's Ellen?"

His father didn't answer, but Will saw a look of pain cross his face. He didn't know.

The second, non-sedated Megalodon had to be almost upon them, and Will was afraid. Were Sir Mallory and the green-suited men ready? Did they have their spears? Was the same thing going to happen again tonight, in the pitch-black, as this afternoon?

Will doubted it, but he'd never know without disobeying his father and looking out the bridge windows.

His stomach lurched as the ship tilted even more with the rush of water coming at them. Will cursed under his breath. His dad could suck it right now. He wasn't going to die without knowing, and he wasn't going to drown without trying to swim and survive if the ship upturned.

He stood and ran to the window, but his dad said nothing. He was pulling the wheel hard, fully concentrating.

Will looked at the deck, but couldn't see anything but random movements until he caught a glimpse of his sister, Ellen, and the techie, Caleb, with his arms around her as though protecting her. They lay sideways on the deck, and Will only made Ellen out because of all the people in the world, he probably knew her form best. Or maybe it was sibling connection. Whatever it was, Will was going out there and getting her.

He scampered sideways out the door, his father screaming after him to stop. He sounded furious, but Will kept going. He climbed down the stairs wall and scampered to the part of the deck where he saw Ellen and the techie.

"Ellen!" he called to her, just out of reach.

"Willie! Willie, run, it's coming!"

He turned and saw nothing but black, and then the second Megalodon rammed the side of the ship. Will heard the crunch and bending of metal. The whole boat hopped high into the air, then plopped back into the water right-side up. The air got knocked out of Will on landing on his belly.

That had to be his dad steadying them. It had to be.

Will grabbed Ellen, and she reached for the young techie, but he had slid far out of reach, hanging by one hand from the deck.

"Caleb!" Ellen cried. She wrenched away from Will and ran to him, but before she could reach him, his fingers slipped and Will heard a splash.

"No!" Ellen yelled, bending over as the ship tilted again. There was no sign of Caleb, and Will knew there never would be.

Now the deck was a mess of activity. Sir Mallory and his green-suited men scampered to aim their weapons, and Nancy and the girls readied another net.

It seemed they suspected this might happen.

"Nancy," Sir Mallory called to her as she got close to the edge of the tilted ship. "You're too close. Back off!"

"I can get it. I can get it, trust me!" She dropped the net overboard as the other two girls did, but they then turned and ran, sliding in the continuous hail. Nancy stayed, staring down and over.

"Get back," Sir Mallory tried again.

"I have to tell you when it's coming up. I can do this. Sharks are my specialty. It'll be up any minute and—"

Any minute became right then, because the Megalodon's enormous mouth rose from the side of the ship and, as though to spite Nancy and only her, it seemed to bend its head and proceeded to chomp Nancy down in its cavernous maw. Will watched in terror as the Megalodon kept its head above water to chew, tilting it up just so, as if it wanted them all to see what it could do.

Her red curls tumbled out of her hood and filled the monstrous shark's teeth. Nancy screamed awful sounds, and Will saw her arms and legs become gored from her body in those horrid, opening and closing rows of teeth. Finally, her head exploded from one ferocious bite, and the cries of pain and begging for mercy stopped. Blood squirted all over the glistening white shark's mouth.

"Now!" Sir Mallory and the green-suited men instantly fired, pulled out the dart guns, and fired again.

The Megalodon struggled. It didn't want to go down like the first one. Maybe the taste of human flesh invigorated it. It rammed the ship again, but with less force, the sedatives starting to take effect. The ship still almost toppled, but Will's dad steered them straight.

Both of Nancy's girls were crying, covering their faces, but Sir Mallory wasn't deterred. "Nancy will not have died in vain!" he cried out. "She believed in this! We will take this Megalodon, too, to the enclosure. The Drake Passage may be full of them! We must get to Elephant Island as soon as possible."

The second Megalodon started to swim in place, as complacent as the first one had been earlier. Sir Mallory went to each girl and told her to take it easy, that he had it from here. With help from the green-suited men, he got the second Megalodon to the back of the ship with the first, side-by-side in a V with their faces close to each other, swimming in trance along with the ship. There was no way they could tow one Megalodon, and certainly not two. The zombie dust somehow made them swim at pace with the ship, not too slow or fast.

Will hoped nobody ever used the zombie powder on him.

He'd never seen anything like Nancy's death, and he felt numb. Simply numb. Like, it didn't happen. Like, he hadn't just been sitting with her sharing a special moment. Maybe his father had been right. This was too dangerous.

He looked at his watch. It was almost 2am. They should be at the Elephant Island compound anytime. Maybe then he'd feel safe again, and maybe he'd believe Sir Mallory saying Nancy died for a cause she believed in, not take it to heart.

But he'd watched it, her being eaten alive, heard her terror and pain-filled screams until she was shark meat. What if that was all of their fates?

He met his father on the bridge. He looked older than an hour or so ago. "Thank you for saving your sister," was all he said. He sounded defeated, yet angry.

"What is it, Dad?" Will asked. He just might tell Will, and it felt like he would right then.

"That woman, Nancy. I didn't want anyone to die. But you know what? I knew. I knew deep down we would be sailing into death, death for us, some of us." He rubbed his bloodshot eyes, then softened his voice, not meeting Will's gaze. "You and Ellen will be fine. Mallory has a sound plan."

"Dad, did you know about the Megalodons?"

He shook his head. "It's so long ago, and I was young. I saw things, knew to sail with them. And not to talk about them." He looked at Will. "But I never forgot them."

"I'll never forget them."

"Son, you'll be remembered for them." He smiled.

"You really think that even though two people died tonight, it's going to work out?"

"Two?"

"A techie went over. Caleb. A kid Ellen liked. Into the water, just gone."

His father examined him carefully. "Yes, you'll be remembered."

CHAPTER 8

It was quarter past 4am when the ship was safely docked in a port Sir Mallory had built beside the Megalodon enclosure on Elephant Island. Nobody talked. They went about the routines set out for them in the frigid night. Sir Mallory had warm water rushing in to de-ice the ship at all times, but there was nothing anyone could do about the storm.

There was some damage to the side of the ship where the second Megalodon had rammed, but nothing his dad's boat couldn't handle.

With Nancy and Caleb gone, some of the spark had left with them. The magic. The non-reality. Will felt it.

The green-suited men got the two sedated Megalodons into the enclosure from the ship. The nets were made of a gelatinous material that stretched at the main rope line, and they could maneuver the giant, docile monsters to a place Will had not yet seen, but was nearby. A giant, natural cave.

He was physically and mentally exhausted, but his head was straight and his stomach still. And man, was he hungry, despite the tragedies and excitement.

Sir Mallory told the remaining people in his party and Will's father's crew that he'd take them to the compound through a tunnel next to the ship's bay. He said tomorrow would be the day he'd show them all the Megalodon enclosure, and they'd broadcast the sharks. Nancy and Caleb would be heroes.

Outside, though, the storm raged on, undeterred by anyone in the group's plans. It had its own ways to follow, its own winds to blow.

The tunnel to the compound was lined ceiling-to-floor with white marble. It led to a black marble room with dozens of colored rugs, and a fountain with a mermaid spilling water from a shell into the pool below in the center of the room. Some of the most comfortable-looking couches and chairs sat all around, and tables engraved with silver and gold etchings rested between and around them. Three chandeliers with at least two dozen lights each hung from the cavernous, molded ceiling.

Sir Mallory said, "Up the stairs there, you'll find the rooms. There are four dozen. Choose as you will. We all need rest. We've fought, and lost great people. Let's dream of them, and let's dream of them when we first saw them."

He looked worn, and went up the steps, Lady Katherine behind him with eyes cast down. People followed, not looking back.

Will watched them go. He still wasn't sleepy and all he could think about was food. He knew from past trips that the minute his body adjusted to joyous land, he felt like Popeye after eating a can of spinach. And he had a lot to think about. He didn't want to do it alone in a bed. He wanted to do it over a ham and cheese with globs of mayo.

He was aware enough to duck behind a large palm plant by the staircase when his dad walked up, because he looked around and asked Ellen where Will was. Ellen shrugged and said Will was probably asleep. He'd seen a lot.

He appreciated that they thought he was fragile, and maybe he was, but they had no idea how good it felt to be on solid, hard-packed, non-moving earth. Nothing could keep him away from finding the ten-million-dollar kitchen and devouring every morsel of goodness he could land a hand on.

He shed his layers of coats and clothes on a red velvet sofa after everyone was gone, and explored. He went down another white marble hallway with a sharp right turn. He took it without looking. It led to another sharp turn, this time to the left. What was this, a funhouse?

This hall was short, and at the end stood a steel door, locked with a keypad. *Hmm.*

He went back to the main room, looked around. Found another hallway, this one lined with finely polished wood panels and floors. Lamps lit the passageway to an ornate wooden door with a silver doorknob. Will turned it and pushed the door open.

More like a zillion-dollar kitchen!

Will ran from cabinet-hiding food storage spot to the next, muttering, "Yes! No! Yeah, maybe!" but never actually making a decision until every nook and cranny had been observed. He settled on what he'd first thought of. A ham and cheese with globs of mayo, but these ingredients were from heaven… He ate two, and then sat back and belched for a solid ten seconds.

It felt so good to be on land. He breathed, cleaned up after himself, and then his mind wandered back to that steel door with the keypad. It's not like the marble hallway was hidden. Anyone could wander that way and find the door. It wouldn't be weird at all if Will asked Sir Mallory about it, a thing in plain sight. Would it?

He wandered back to the lush main room and lounged on a golden, soft loveseat, propping his feet on a hand-carved coffee table. This was the life, but it was kind of boring. He felt restless, had put off thinking about the deaths earlier, and just wanted to roam, feel the earth, be alone for the first time in ages.

He decided to go back down the first white marble tunnel to the boat dock.

He wasn't wearing his layers, so he stayed close to the door, and only for a minute. He examined the dock as well as he could. There was a curve to the wall of the island that must be one side of the cave holding the Megalodons.

Will's curiosity piqued. He couldn't make it to that curve or he'd freeze to death, but there had to be some way into the enclosure. He could find it, sneak a glimpse tonight.

If he dared.

And he did.

He went back down the marble hallway and to the main room. He studied the six walls, all with doors or halls leading off them. Then there was the staircase on a seventh wall.

One hall led to the kitchen, another to the boat dock, and the weird one led to the locked steel door, leaving two Will hadn't explored.

One was directly beside the white marble hallway to the boat dock, and it had a subtle look to it. A simple light wood with carvings of starfish, and a nice brass handle. With a big, old-fashioned keyhole.

A keypad was something Will could not crack, but this? All he needed was a small fork, and the everything-stocked kitchen had any tool he could ask for. He headed that way, returning with a few pieces that might do the trick.

Within ten minutes, the lock clicked and Will turned the doorknob. He looked inside.

The walls were carved from the rock of the island and polished to a high shine, with track lighting on the floors and ceilings. Will went into the hallway and followed its natural rock curve to what he hoped was the Megalodons' enclosure. It was a long hall, but his wishes paid off as he entered a softly lit, enormous room the size of three football fields, a cave formed in the rock made perfectly for this. Lights under water showed how deep it went, so deep the bottom couldn't be seen. Once on far side of the enclosure, Will saw the open sea, snow falling there. Giant metal bars blocked the way out. On the other side, the cave simply rounded out.

It was chilly inside. The sharks had to be kept cold, perhaps. But it wasn't freezing. As Will's eyes adjusted to the soft lighting and he scanned the water for a Megalodon, he heard a voice.

"You couldn't rest, either, could you, Will?" It was Sir Mallory's accent and voice, but soft, subdued as before.

He looked to his right and saw Sir Mallory standing at the edge of a thick metal fence between the Megalodon enclosure and the walkway the hall led out onto. "No."

"Why not?"

"It's being on land, I think. It feels so good, I want to be awake, do something. Oh, I really wanted to eat. I had two sandwiches earlier. Your kitchen is great, I mean, great." He'd been so shocked that he wasn't alone that he'd babbled. Plus, he didn't like seeing Sir Mallory this way, so down.

To his surprise, Sir Mallory turned to him with a slight grin. "You do have a rejuvenating spirit, don't you?"

"What do you mean?" He was puzzled.

"You bounce back, I think some might say. You see the positive, you don't let the hard things, the bad things change who you are. Do you know how rare that is?"

Will shook his head, wondering if he were really that way.

"I'm not surprised you made your way here, although I did lock the door behind me. Come here; stand by me and look down."

Will did, and saw the smaller of the Megalodons, the second one they'd caught, the one who'd taken Nancy. It swam about fifty feet below the surface, idle, seemingly content, its dorsal fin inches from the surface. "Is it asleep?"

"It still has the drugs in its system. They will wear off tomorrow. Don't worry, we have smaller doses if things get out of hand. And these walls, they are enforced with steel bars, all around."

"Wow."

"I'm pleased you approve." He grinned. "You have a way about you. Something unusual, something so casual that being around you makes me feel young, free. Thank you."

He didn't know what to say, so he looked down at the Megalodon again, watching its swishing, giant white tail. Back and forth, so slowly, back and forth.

Its mouth with those teeth were below it, out of sight. Mouth closed? Most likely. Will knew it only opened its mouth when it fed. Knew it.

There were other, bigger fish swimming in the water enclosure, too. "What are those for?"

"We'll feed them to the Megalodons. Freed the giants from the nets as soon as they were locked up. They haven't come out of their stupors enough to feed, but they will. That's the first thing they'll do. We'll be watching. There's a deep underwater current into this cave, and we widened the bars enough for the natural habitat wildlife to come through for the Megalodons to feed on. And we'll watch." He pointed around the ceilings of the room. Cameras were mounted everywhere. Then he pointed below the water near the lights. More cameras. Underwater, special cameras.

He continued. "We have a study with monitors on the entire enclosure on the other side of the compound. It is always manned by two people, sometimes more."

"Why?"

"Safety. These are deadly, ancient, and we know nothing of their methods or ways. We have to take utmost care or what happened to Nancy and Caleb might happen again." His face fell. "I regret that. I won't let it happen again."

"You tried to stop her."

He nodded, but stared down at the sedated Megalodon.

"Caleb was nowhere near you. That was just pure accident, the ocean, the force…"

"You're right, I know you are. It still eats at me." He looked at Will. "May I ask you a personal question?"

"Sure."

"How did your mother die?"

He paused. Not what he expected. "She had a brain tumor. She died fast."

"How old were you?"

"Two."

"You don't remember her at all?"

"No."

He smiled. "Thank you for being so honest and forthcoming. I have one more question. Were your mother and father deeply in love?"

Will nodded his head, meeting Sir Mallory's eyes. "Everyone tells me they were. Dad's never dated anyone else."

"To be so in love, both of you together. A team, comrades for life." He patted Will's head. "Now, before we freeze, let's go to our bedchambers. Sleep is important. Dreams are a must. They cure everything, just like a glass of ice water."

CHAPTER 9

Will's belly rumbled so loudly that it woke him from his satin sheets and he bolted upright. He'd fallen asleep in his boating clothes. Better clean up fast so he could eat as soon as possible. He was even hungrier than the night before.

He had planned to go straight to the kitchen, but everybody was in the main black marble hall. Eating! There were three men in white coats serving them off of silver platters.

"Willie!" Ellen called, waving at him. She sat at the base of a huge flaming hearth Will hadn't noticed the night before. Probably because it was made of black marble.

He joined her. "They bring it to me? Anything?"

"You'll want everything." She smiled, but her eyes didn't match. Her cheeks were hollow.

Most sat in twos and threes, but Lady Katherine ate alone in a chair with one table.

The siblings ate in silence, Will wondering where his dad and Sir Mallory were.

At last, the pair of them emerged from the only door Will hadn't probed the night before. Sir Mallory seemed distressed, and Will's dad downright pissed.

"What is it?" Don Mack asked.

"Storm," was all Will's father said.

Sir Mallory waved his hands around. "No transmissions with the weather like this. We can't get or send a signal."

"How bad is the storm?" one of Nancy's girls asked.

"It'll last a few days, fierce and unyielding," said Will's dad.

Sir Mallory rested his hand on Will's father's shoulder. "We'll wait it out. We've come a long way, all of us, from around the world. But, for now, I'd like to invite all of you to come see them, the Megalodons. They are more alert, and we expect them to start feeding in the next couple hours. Do come." He glanced at Will's dad, who rubbed his tired face. Will got the feeling his father still hadn't slept.

Everybody rose at once, slipping on heavy coats, but Sir Mallory told them just normal cold weather clothing would be just fine. Will remembered how the enclosure had felt the night before, cool, not frigid like the raging storm outside. Sir Mallory must have some kind of heating system in place for it.

Sir Mallory's people, Will's father and crew, and Will and Ellen all filed through the wooden door with the brass doorknob and down the cave hall. Will couldn't wait to see them again, excitement hitting him anew. He knew they'd all be safe from the monstrous sharks; he'd already seen the safety measures. Bars in the cave walls, for crying out loud.

Once all of them were in the enclosure, they lined up in the walkway, faces pointed down through the thick steel bars to the water. Daylight spilled in, dark and gloomy from the blizzard, from beyond the barred cave entrance. Will noticed the green-suited men at four different spots away from the rest of them in the enclosure, already having been there. They just wore their green suits now. Will thought they must be military. Each held a dart gun at the ready, loaded with zombie dust, Will assumed, just in case.

In case of what?

The two Megalodons swam in lazy circles around each other about thirty feet below the surface. They still seemed dazed to Will, but Sir Mallory had said it would be a couple hours before they were ready to begin feeding.

How much sea life would it take to feed both of these creatures? He couldn't imagine there would ever be enough, but there were plenty of large fish in the water with them, seemingly unaware of the predators' intentions whenever they stopped playing ring around the rosy.

Nobody spoke; they watched.

"I didn't want to see them again," Ellen said low in Will's right ear.

"The danger is over," he told her, confident.

"I don't know how you can be so…so…so normal after last night. You saw what I saw. I tried to sleep, but kept waking up, seeing that poor woman with the red hair…and Caleb…" She turned her back on the sharks and put her head down.

"Hey, it's okay." Will tried to console her, putting a hand on her arm. "Last night was an accident, for both Nancy and Caleb. No, it wasn't supposed to happen that way, but it did, and we're here, and this is just how it is. But nothing else bad is going to happen."

She huffed and glared at him. "God, you sound like Dad. This happened and now we're here and that's that. No feelings, no thoughts, just look at the giant killer sharks." She ran to the hall leading to the compound, leaving Will feeling stupid. He never knew the right thing to say.

"I still think we should keep the tetrodotoxin in their systems until the satellite signal comes back," Will's father said, breaking the hush of the group.

"Why the hell aren't we?" Don Mack asked, his black, greasy hair a mess around his head. He hadn't even bothered combing it when he left his room after sleeping, but such was Don Mack at his best.

"Too much tetrodotoxin might kill them. I explained this to Captain Miller," Sir Mallory said. "They can asphyxiate and die if they are too sedated from the stuff. Their very hearts will stop."

Lady Katherine pulled a camera out of her purse and started taking pictures of the sharks. "Now, my dear, we have your proof. On my camera."

Sir Mallory put his arm around her and kissed the top of her head. "Tell me this doesn't thrill you at least a little."

Her mouth stayed tight as always, neither smiling nor frowning, making her impossible to read. "I'm just here because it was so important to you. I know we need the live feed, and I know they need to be active."

"This is active enough," Will's father insisted, rubbing the black whip on his hip.

"They have to eat. Their sheer size! They must eat, and a lot, or they'll grow weak, and fast," Sir Mallory countered. "We have to at least let them get some normalcy back enough to feed. Captain

Miller, you have been more than understanding, so I promise you that if they become too awfully aggressive, we'll sedate them again. Just to a lesser degree than when we had to bring them to the island, to keep them from death."

Will watched his father's gaze following the bigger of the two giant sharks. He had circles under his brown eyes and hadn't changed clothes at all in days. He usually took better care of himself on land, admittedly letting himself go a bit when he was sailing. It worried Will.

"Let's go back," said Lady Katherine. "I'm getting a chill and could use some tea. I'm sure we all could, don't you think?"

"Yes, wonderful idea, Katty," Sir Mallory said to her, and she turned and went the same way Ellen had gone, head held high, eyes cast down.

They all followed, Will leaving last with a glance around at the green-suited men and their dart guns. He hadn't been ready to go, to stop watching the tamed monsters from an era long gone. They were true magic in a world where kids his age found magic in their fantasy video games.

Once in the main black marble room again, people settled down to rest and drink beverages of their choosing, brought to them from the men in white suits. Ellen was nowhere to be seen, and Will assumed she must have gone back to her room. He hated that the night before affected her so much. Couldn't she see how amazing all this was, see past the misfortune and to the bigger picture?

He decided there wasn't anything he could do at that point for Ellen, and he wanted to know what was behind the door he hadn't checked out the night before. He approached it and knocked.

"Come on in," a British accent called. James.

Will opened the door to a large, circular room full of monitors and tech equipment. James swiveled in his chair away from one screen showing a Megalodon circling and said, "Hello, young fellow. You're a curious one. Sir Mallory told me you made it to the enclosure last night. Missed us in here, though. Did you shake the whole palace down but my nook of the woods?" Now that James wasn't all covered up, Will saw he had red hair, pale skin, and a thin frame. He wore jeans and a sweater.

"How'd you know?"

"I've been in here since we arrived. Need a snooze soon, don't you think?"

The other tech guy in the room yawned and said, "Double that. Kid, why don't you take over for us?"

Will's eyes widened. "I wouldn't…I mean, I have no idea…"

They both chuckled. James said, "Just kidding, mate. Our relief duo should be taking over any minute. Why don't you watch with them for a bit? Might learn something."

Will doubted it. Machines weren't his specialty, but come to think of it, Will didn't have any specialties to speak of, anyway.

A man and a woman came in behind Will and the techies made jokes and traded shifts. Will faded out of the room and back to the main hall. Less people were there now. He didn't see his father, so maybe his dad was actually getting sleep for the first time in three days. He hoped so. He wanted his dad to be in a better mood for this.

He felt awkward approaching any of the crew or Sir Mallory's people, having never really talked to them before, and there was nobody in the room he could sit with to pass the time until the Megalodons fed. And that was certainly what he was waiting for.

Not even Don Mack showed his mug in the small group of people scattered around.

He wished he hadn't ticked off Ellen.

Will sat by the fire and thought of what he could do. He knew what he wanted to do. He wanted to go watch the Megalodons regain their minds, even if it did take two hours. He could watch them forever. But in a room of adults, much different from the night before, he felt like he needed to ask permission to go to the enclosure. There simply was nobody to ask but Lady Katherine, and she made him uncomfortable. Still, the longer he sat by the fire thinking about how he was a few dozen yards away from prehistoric sharks, the more he got up the nerve to approach Lady Katherine.

She sat in the same small chair as earlier with a book. Will looked at the cover while waiting for her to notice him standing in front of her. It bore a red cardinal on a black background and the title *She Walks Alone* on it.

Just when he was losing his nerve, she said, "Yes?" without looking up. "What is it you need?"

"Ma'am, uh, Lady Katherine, can I go watch the Megalodons?"

She put her book facedown in her lap and squinted up at him. "My, you are tall for twelve. Jeffery sees himself in you, I assume, but I can't imagine why." She smiled. "He didn't grow tall until he was fifteen, or so he says."

Will fidgeted under her scrutiny, unsure if she was being nice or messing with him. He decided to wait and see what she said next, but she sat there staring for a long time. He kept his eyes down.

"No, you're not really like him. You're like your father." She picked up the book with the cardinal on it and said, "I don't see why not."

"Wait, what do you mean?"

She put the book down again, tilted her head at him, and said, "Go on, watch the sharks. You need not my permission." Back to the book.

He all but ran to the starfish-carved door and down the cave hall to the enclosure.

Once inside, the green-suited men all gave him nods, but none spoke to him. They kept alert eyes on the water.

Will sat down in front of the bars blocking him from the sharks and looked down into the water. They still swam in a yin-yang pattern with each other, but their tails seemed to swish with a little more fever. Their long, long white bodies arched and stretched around each other as though dancing a dance that should have been extinct with them. Will was mesmerized.

So enraptured was he that he forgot time, forgot about the deaths the night before, forgot the feeling that his father thought he was a weak kid who couldn't sail without getting sick.

When the Megalodons swam higher in the water, Will thought nothing of it except to be enticed that he might see more details about them. They continued circling, but faster, tails whipping like storms every once in a while, making the surface of the water splash.

Will's attention was pulled away when he noticed what looked like eight or nine huge fish swimming at lightning speed from the back of the enclosure to the bars at the entrance, skimming the surface and going around the Megalodons. But they were too slow.

The Megalodons had awakened.

The larger of the two lunged out of the circling formation, huge mouth gaping, giant teeth distorted by the disturbed waters. Its head came right out of the water, fish in its jaws, and Will fell back from the stench coming off its breath. It splashed back down into the water, blood spraying everywhere, including onto Will's face. The smaller Megalodon took note; another thrust upward from this one, the foul odor filling the chamber when it clamped down on its prey at the surface. The fish stood no chance. It was demolished in a swallow. The shark didn't even chew it.

Will sat back up, eyes wide with excitement, now ignoring the death scent that came with the creatures' open maws. He watched as the pair decimated the small group of fish, and the lights in the water reflected red blood.

A green-suited man about forty yards away near the front of the enclosure yelled to the other men, "Be ready."

Ready for what?

Those smaller fish really weren't a meal for the giant aquatic beasts, and they became agitated, or so it seemed to Will. They swam all around now, to the front and then to the back, separate from one another. Will couldn't keep up with them. They were feeding on deeper sea life, and the water just got redder, murkier, until Will couldn't see the Megalodons at all anymore.

He stood up and leaned his forehead against the bars, looking hard into the water to see something, anything.

A long, thin white fin came up out of the blood-filled water, but beyond that, Will couldn't see the rest of the beast. He held his breath, unable to move, unable to breathe as the fin came closer to him, not too fast, not too slow, red dripping down the perfect white. The surface of the water was ten feet lower than the base of the enclosure walkway, but the dorsal fin rose high into the enclosure, with light from the open side of the cave making it glisten and shine like a knife.

He was safe; the shark couldn't get him behind these bars. Out of the corner of his eye, he saw the same green-suited man coming toward him, but right then, the Megalodon whose fin had been coming surged out from under the surface of the bloody water, mouth gaping, jagged rows of sharp, huge teeth filling Will's entire vision until the shark smashed into the bars right in front of Will.

Shock and fear filled him as the creature's reek enveloped him.

Will fell on his butt, and frantically scooted backward until his backbone was against the wall. He still kept pushing into the wall as the shark charged again at the bars where he'd been standing, and Will could see straight down its throat, just past the teeth, right before he closed his eyes instinctively to the stinking breath. He heard it hit the bars again, and the ground under him shook.

He opened his eyes. Two fins now rose high from the red mess of water, one a little shorter than the other, and Will could imagine them just under the surface in front of him, swimming side-by-side, trying to figure out best how to get through those bars and to Will's sweet, small snack of a body.

His heart pounded, and even though it was chilly in the cave, he felt sweat all over his body like he had a sudden fever, and his skin flushed hot. He had one thought—run.

CHAPTER 10

As long as Will could remember, Ellen had taken care of him. His father was often at sea, and when the kids weren't in school, he took them on every sailing trip he was hired for. Their main home base was a two-story white house on the coast in Virginia where their dad could get quick jobs during bad weather seasons in one of the planet's hurricane favorites.

Ellen had always been good to him, but she made him do everything for himself from a young age. "If I can do it for myself, you can do it for yourself. Come on. You're not an idiot."

It taught him to make decisions more quickly than most kids his age, and perhaps many adults never learn this skill.

His decision to run from the gargantuan, sharp-toothed, reeking mouth shaking the floor of the cave in its bashing attempt to get him was instantaneous, but some other thing took hold of him. He couldn't move. He was actually scared stiff, unable to make his body follow the run command.

Two green-suited men were in front of him in seconds, shooting from two sides into the Megalodon's gills with the dart guns.

The shark swung its head from side-to-side, exposed to the air and filling it with its putrid smell, as though fighting the zombie dust, somehow knowing...and then it submerged into the murky and bloody water of the enclosure.

And then Will ran.

Everybody was in the main hall. They'd seen what happened on the cameras. Will dashed past all of them, not looking, not caring. He took the stairs two at a time, and went into a random room all the way at the farthest point in the hallway of rooms. It looked unused.

He climbed into the lush bed and pulled his knees up to his chest, wrapping his arms around them. He couldn't believe he'd frozen like that.

He also couldn't believe he'd found something that absolutely terrifying in the world, and it had happened to him.

Will didn't know how long he sat like that, nor when he began rocking back and forth like he was trying to keep warm. Those teeth…that god-awful smell of the Megalodon's breath. If those bars hadn't separated Will from the giant prehistoric shark, he would have simply been so scared stiff that he would have been shark food.

Those teeth crunching him up like he'd seen them do with the fish…like with Nancy…the unbearable pain he would have felt, begging for the end as the Megalodon chewed him to pieces alive.

He ran a hand through his short hair, then down his face, ever so slowly. He wasn't going to allow what happened earlier shake him, nor would he fail to react if anything like that happened again. What if something out there on Elephant Island went wrong and they all were at the mercy of the water giants? Will had to grow some balls in the face of the magnificent and deadly Megalodons.

He didn't know how long he'd been sitting upright and fetal, rocking back and forth, but the door to the bedroom opened and he snapped his head up, heart pounding all over again.

It was just Ellen.

"How did you find me?" he asked her.

She closed the door behind her, went to the windows, and opened the drapes. Blinding white light of a daytime snowstorm of the coldest degree filled the room, making Will squint. She turned to him with her hands on her hips. "I saw what happened to you on the monitors. A bunch of us did. Why didn't you stop when we called out for you?"

Will looked at his knees and didn't answer. It had been a childish way to act when he so wanted to prove he wasn't a kid anymore.

Ellen came to the bed and sat down next to Will, stretching her legs out in front of her. She gently rubbed Will's back with her fingernails. "It looked terrifying."

"Yeah."

"I mean, it was so close to you. I was really afraid. I knew nothing could happen, but for a split-second, I was sure you were…you know. Just a split-second, like I said." Ellen pushed her hair out of her face with her free hand, looking at her feet.

"Sorry I freaked. I should have stopped when I heard people calling for me. I just…needed to be alone, needed to think."

"It scared the shit out of you, didn't it?" She turned her head to him, and he reluctantly met her eyes.

"Yeah, yeah it did. But don't tell Dad. If he thinks I'm freaked, he'll ship us all out. I'm okay now, though. I had to think about it, figure out what I would do if it happened again."

"You just sat there for so long." She frowned.

"I know, I know. I froze up, couldn't think, couldn't move. It won't happen again. I know what to do now."

Ellen sighed. "You don't have the instincts to change your natural reactions, that's something you have to learn."

"Well, I think I just had a crash course." He grinned at her, trying to lighten the mood, but it didn't work.

In a soft voice, Ellen said, "They scare me. Ever since Nancy, but the first time I saw them feed, all that blood. I mean, so much freaking blood. Those big, poor fish were massacred. I don't know, maybe I'm squeamish, but I actually have started hating them, this whole expedition." She looked back to her feet. "Don't tell Dad."

"I don't feel that way."

"How do you feel?"

He shrugged, trying to find the words. Finally, he said, "It's the adventure, I guess. And they amaze me, even though one just about made me crap my pants. Even the feeding doesn't get to me. At first, all the blood was weird, but they are giant sharks. Of course, they're going to spread a bunch of blood into the water. There's more, though. I think Dad thinks more of me. He likes to see some spirit in me, something we can relate about."

"You think Dad's into this?"

"Oh, yeah. Don Mack told me stories about him from when he was younger, before Mom."

"What? Tell me!" she insisted.

Will gave her the rundown of Don Mack's tales, including their father's deadeye with a gun. Ellen oooed and ahhhed.

"There's so much to him that we don't know," she told Will. "He's all quiet, but there's a lot under the surface. I'd always known he was a good sailor, but what he did when the Megalodons came was out of this world."

"Yeah, it really was."

They smiled at each other.

"They sedated the Megalodons after what happened to you. Sir Mallory said not too much, that they needed to feed later tonight. Dad insisted. I'm glad Sir Mallory listens to Dad."

"Me too."

She patted his arm. "Are you feeling a little better after a talk with your big sis who somehow psychically knew which room you'd hidden away in?"

"Yeah, I am. But I think I'm going to stay in here a little longer. I feel so tired."

"Get under these fancy covers and sleep! You need it. You never rest on a boat, and your schedule is all wacky." She got off the bed, smoothing her sweatshirt out. "I'll let you get to it. Love you, Willie."

"Love you, too."

She left, and Will took her advice by snuggling up in the covers of the soft bed and almost immediately fell asleep.

Will had been pretty much all but dead, but when the walls and foundation of his bedroom shook like lightning had struck, he popped out of bed, wide-eyed and breathing heavily. Sweat covered his body and he felt chilled, but he didn't remember dreaming anything that would have his body in this state.

Had he imagined the shaking, pounding burst in his room? It was completely dark, even though Ellen had left the drapes open. What time was it?

Then again, there it was! Boom! Everything shook, and a couple framed paintings fell off a far wall.

Will shoved the covers off and jumped out of bed. He had to get downstairs and find out what was happening.

Once in the main hall, he saw everyone crowded around the computer room, except for Ellen, Don Mack, and some of the crew. He pushed his way to the front without asking questions because the smashing, shaking pounds hit again, and what was the point of asking when he could simply go see what had everyone's attention? It was clearly something with the Megalodons, and it wasn't good.

The biggest monitor's camera hung overhead the entire shark enclosure, and Will saw the two enormous water beasts near the surface, but one was on the east wall, and the other was on the west wall. They swam in tight circles. God, they were big.

He watched as, at the same time, they both swam to the middle of the water, turned, and their tails moved harder and faster than motor blades, projecting them to the very walls themselves.

Everything shook again as the monster sharks struck the hard rock cave walls. Will heard trinkets and drinking glasses fall off tables in the black marble hall. He had to grip Mallory's shoulder to keep from falling.

"Sedate them again," Will's father said, almost casually. "Storm's still too much for signal."

Mallory waited, thinking. "But they have to eat. And it would distract them from…this."

James piped in. "I've noticed something. Watching them do this, it's almost like they're planning it out, looking for a weakness. Yeah?"

"Sedate them," Will's father repeated.

"They'll get too weak…" Sir Mallory rubbed his chin.

"You have a way to feed them that doesn't rely on what fits through your bars?" Will's dad asked Sir Mallory.

"I have a stocked food supply for them in which food can be delivered through an entrance underwater in the enclosure."

"Do that, then sedate them. They're going to shake this place to pieces," he replied, then shifted to the side and grabbed the doorway as the huge sharks hit the walls again. One of Nancy's girls yelped. Will was smashed between swaying bodies and just went with it.

"Yes, that's what we'll do. I'll lightly sedate them for the rest of the night. Can't give them too much, as you know. It'll be plenty to keep them from doing…that again. We'll let them feed in the day tomorrow again, too." He turned and hurried to the doorway leading to the enclosure.

Will couldn't help himself. "I'm going, too." He wanted to face the beasts again while they were aggressive, prove to himself that he could keep from getting scared to death.

"Like hell," his father said.

Will shrugged at him. "Stop me." He ran after Mallory, hearing his father follow with hard, heavy footsteps on the marble floor.

Once in the enclosure, Will caught up to Sir Mallory just as the enormous sharks bashed the walls again. This close to the action, Will had to fall back against the cave wall to keep his balance, not fall down. Mallory grabbed the steel bars as Will's dad reached them, gripping the doorway with both hands as everything rumbled violently.

Sir Mallory wasn't shaken. All four of the green-suited men were there with their dart guns. Did they ever sleep?

"We need to release food from the storage compartment," Sir Mallory said to the closest green-suited man. He nodded and spoke into a walkie-talkie. Will couldn't make out what he said.

He inched up to the bars. The Megalodons swam in those tight circles, making the surface water ragged and swirly. Foam sprung around their dorsal fins, which stuck high out of the water, white and gleaming, ready to be blood-stained again.

Will couldn't see the food door open, but the sharks' behavior changed quite suddenly. Will's father joined him and Sir Mallory at the bars as the Megalodons lined up with their heads facing the back of the cave wall, fins straight and steady. Will could see their black, gigantic eyes were brighter, and perhaps madder from banging their heads against stone and starving.

The feeding instantly began when a school of about fifty large deep-sea fish became visible at the surface of the water in front of the sharks. Both of the monsters pumped their tails like they had when ramming the cave walls, and off they went toward the unsuspecting fish food.

The bigger Megalodon made the first kill by filling its mouth with two fish at the same time, rising its head out of the water, teeth popping out around them, and then crunching them to pieces. Blood sprayed through the air as the horrid scent of the Megalodon's breath hit Will. He covered his nose. The Megalodon submerged again in a well of bloody water as the other shark struck, this time under water. It was a true savage, snapping at fish swimming in a panic, not bothering to kill and eat them one or two at a time like the other Megalodon. This one, from what Will could make out as the water got redder, wanted to damage and incapacitate as many victims as possible, and then gorge itself.

Finally, the wild surface of the now pitch-red water settled after what felt to Will like both a couple minutes and an hour. He saw nothing but two dorsal fins sticking out of the water, going in circles like before the feeding frenzy. The normally shining white fins were streaked with blood water, like the last time they fed.

And then, all at once, they both made dashes for the walls again, hitting them with so much force that Will fell down. The whole cave vibrated, making disastrous sounds. Will's father grabbed him up, asking if he was alright.

"Yeah." He was embarrassed that he'd lost his balance, but proud he could watch the feeding.

Will's father turned to Sir Mallory. "Now you sedate them. Look at them. They're still doing it."

Mallory nodded, frowning. He signaled the green-suited men and they got their dart guns ready. The closest one called out, "Gonna be hard with the water this cloudy. Gotta get a gill."

Mallory thought for a moment. "We'll release a few more fish, and when they come up to feed, shoot them. But not with too much. They have to stay alive."

More fish must've entered from the storage area, because the fins lined up, and soon they both were poking their gigantic heads out of the water, teeth popping out, and snatching up fishies. The green suit men were on it, and Will admired their skills. Two misses, but two dead-on hits to the gills from two men, and slowly, the sharks slowed down into swimming in big, lazy circles in the bloody water.

Once again, they were sedated.

Sir Mallory turned to Will. "You did well. I'm impressed. You had been scared earlier, and you faced your fears."

"And you have blood on your cheek," Will's father grumbled while licking his thumb, and then wiping Will's cheekbone. Will hadn't even felt it hit him.

"You have some on your shirt, Dad," Will said, noticing a red splatter pattern on his father's plaid flannel.

Mallory grinned at them. "You two, why don't you watch them together for a bit? Well, their lazy and giant fins, anyway. After all, the bond you share made all this possible."

Will smiled at Sir Mallory as he winked and left down the cave hall and away. Suddenly, Will felt nervous being alone with his dad. This was, indeed, the most unusual situation they'd ever been in together, the whole trip included.

His father leaned against the bars and watched, breaking the silence with, "Sharks usually strike from behind. These, though, will go at anything from any angle. Some sharks drown their food before eating it, too, but these don't. That little one, the way it ripped those fish up enough to disable them, and then going back for them…that's not shark behavior. Not that I know of."

"Do you know a lot about sharks?"

He nodded slowly. "I've even killed them. For sport, and for kill or be killed. They are sensitive at the tip of their noses. These two, I've noticed, ram the walls with the tops of their heads. Their noses must be sensitive like other sharks'. A crack off my whip on a shark's nose can be enough to stun it solid. I wonder…if on these…."

Will said nothing and imagined a young version of his father with half a bottle of whiskey in one hand, and alternating firing off shots and waving his whip at sea sharks with the other. He didn't want to know about any times his dad was almost killed by a shark, not particularly now right after seeing the Megalodons feed.

"You okay with all this, Will?" he asked, looking down at him.

"Oh, yeah, Dad. Nothing like this has ever happened to me. Nothing like it ever will. I feel…"

"You feel what?" He sounded genuinely curious, not ready to criticize. It made Will feel like he could try to express himself honestly.

"I want to be around them, see what they do. They're so big! I mean, big. Even the feeding is exciting to me. I didn't like it when they were pounding on the walls, but Sir Mallory fixed that. I think we're going to be okay, that after this storm, we'll make history and maybe even change the way people think somehow. Know what I mean?"

His father chuckled and gazed back at the fins rising high and circling slowly. "I do."

The watched in silence together for a while, and then his father said, "We should eat. Then to bed. Maybe tomorrow the weather will be better."

"Okay." They both turned to leave, but suddenly they heard…something. It was as though something scratched on the other side of the back of the cave enclosure. Like rock being chewed by diamond teeth.

"Dad, what was that?"

He stared at the far wall. "I don't know."

"I don't like it. Are there more caves? Is there one behind that wall?"

"I don't know, but this is an island, and islands are, by their nature of formation, full of caves. Come, son, let's get out of here and tell the techies. They must be able to figure out something with all the gadgets they have."

Will felt uneasy, a deep, sinking feeling in his gut as though something unknown and very bad was about to happen. "Okay, Dad. Let's go." Truth was, even though he could stay with the Megalodons forever, that odd scraping sound on the other side of the enclosure wall spooked him.

They left walking side-by-side, and quickly.

CHAPTER 11

None of the tech heads had any clue what Will and his father heard, and James suggested it could have been wildlife living in the caves of the island responding to the Megalodons' banging on the walls. Will didn't feel satisfied with that answer.

He wasn't tired after sleeping so long, so he ate two ham sandwiches in the kitchen. The tuxedoed servers were off-duty and asleep, most likely. The sandwiches, where they had been scrumptious when Will had them the first day they arrived, were tasteless and mainly just sustenance.

When finished eating and dishes cleaned up, Will went into the main hall to see if anybody else was awake. Only Sir Mallory was there, sitting in the same chair his wife had been glued to most of the time. He was administering a shot into his bare hip, and glanced up at Will as he pulled the needle out. "See?" he said. "Insulin shot. Not nearly as bad as it looks. To do, I mean, especially after doing so all my life." He wrapped the needle up in paper towels, carried it over to a waste bin, and chucked it. "Sit with an old man, Will. I can't sleep, and it looks like you can't, either. Visit the food storage, did you?"

"Yeah."

"Good eats?"

"Yeah, all the food here is great," Will said, even though he hadn't enjoyed his sandwiches.

"Come," Sir Mallory said. "Let's sit by the fire."

Will joined him on the black marble fireplace as he lit a cigar, blowing out slowly. "You don't mind, do you?" he asked, gesturing to the cigar.

"No. Dad smokes cigarettes sometimes."

"Just sometimes?"

"Yeah."

"Well, that's something. Cigarettes, well, most people can't have them only sometimes. They fiend for them until they break the cycle. Your father has willpower. Maybe that's why he named you Will." He smiled.

Will smiled back at him, not explaining that his mother had named him William after her father, who had died when she was a teen. "Dad's pretty much his own man."

"That he is, that he is. A cigar, on the other hand, is a treat. Something one puffs on after a long day or at a tedious dinner party to get a break from the socialites."

"What is it right now?"

Sir Mallory paused, thinking. "I'll be honest with you, Will. In this case, it's to soothe the nerves. Much like a cigarette might." He puffed, paused, and then continued. "I worry that this storm will never clear, that we'll never get satellite signal out, and that the Megalodons' existence will never be known."

Will thought that was so very honest, and felt honored that the Englishman talked to him yet again like an equal, like an adult. "I don't think that will happen," he reassured Sir Mallory instinctively, but in his gut, he remembered those odd sounds at the back of the cave wall earlier. He didn't bring that up.

"Thank you." He smiled. "Nerves, like I say. And nerves, Will, are simply insecurities that your plans won't work out, that your dreams won't come true…without knowing either way. Isn't that the devil?"

"I guess so. For me, the devil is not being able to sail without feeling like puking the whole time. I hate it."

"Why is that? Is it because you have to do it so much, or because you think you look weak to your father?" Sir Mallory watched him carefully.

Will blushed at the man's insightfulness. His true weakness, which only Ellen knew, had been observed.

"You don't have to answer. I see what it is. Having your father's approval is, perhaps, a boy's most desperate desire. However, you don't see what I see. Do you want to know what I see?"

Will looked at the black marble floor, thinking, and then slowly nodded. "Sure." Sir Mallory was wise, and Will sincerely wanted to know what he thought. He had a way of putting things into perspective with words that were positive and insightful. Things Will couldn't see until pointed out to him that way. Just then, he wished his father talked to him like Sir Mallory did.

"I see your father as a gentle, loving father who doesn't know how to express his love for his children in a way that they know it. And he does. He adores you and your sister. He agreed to this adventure simply because of something you said to him, and I imagine all you expressed to him was a strong desire to do this. Am I right?" he asked.

"Yeah. I guess so. I was angry, though. I wasn't nice about it."

Sir Mallory puffed and leaned closer to him. "Why not nice?"

Will shrugged. "I'm always nice to Dad. I don't ever want to upset him, but that night, I was mad. I wanted to catch a Megalodon, or at least try. I figured the only way I could get him to change his mind was to blow up at him. I got myself worked up and then did it."

"How did he react?"

Will bit his lip, and then replied, "He seemed almost excited."

"What do you think he was excited about?"

"That I wanted to do something at sea. Something he would do without Ellen or me onboard."

"Hmm," Sir Mallory said. Puff. "Maybe he liked seeing your spirit. Maybe he wanted to please you. You see, Will, a father doesn't know how to talk to his son when he has passed childhood and has become more adult. Especially a single father without a woman's advice and insight. And your father, bless him, doesn't seem to know how to show his true feelings. He's a hard man to get to know, and like most sailors, has a gruff outward persona. That's why they crave the sea. The open waters, the calm, being away from everyone. The freedom, the very air of the sea clears the mind."

Will listened and pondered it after Sir Mallory stopped talking. "I never thought of him like that."

"That's for two reasons. One, he's your father, so of course you want approval. Second, you are not a sailor, so you don't understand the draw of the ocean and its way of taking your memories, especially the bad ones, away."

"Dad has some bad ones."

"Yes," Sir Mallory murmured. "Yes, he does."

They sat in silence for a while, Sir Mallory enjoying his cigar, and Will thinking over the conversation. He'd always thought of his father as an unemotional man, one who lost that capacity when Will's mother died. However, what Sir Mallory said hit home as to what might actually motivate Will's father. He'd never thought of the sea as a place to forget, but rather a miserable place where he felt sick all the time and like a broken leg to his father. It wasn't all about him, though, which is what Sir Mallory pointed out to him. His father, although in his late fifties, was still a human, maybe not knowing what to do all the time like Will assumed he did. Maybe he was as confused as the rest of the people in the world as to what to do and not do, and his way of dealing with that was to put forward a tough exterior, and not show weakness. Especially to his kids.

That insight alone made Will appreciate his father more. He couldn't imagine having two teenage kids and raising them alone, not knowing what to say to them or how to make them feel secure about themselves. That didn't go so much for Ellen. Ellen loved being at sea, and she and their father had always had a special bond Will didn't share with his dad. The father-daughter thing. Daddy's little girl.

Will realized Ellen made it easy on their father. She figured out his sensitive side young and how to bring it out. She also seemed to instinctively know that their father was not all grit, but had a gentle side that Will never thought to look for. Instead, he answered his dad's questions like he thought his father would want him to rather than saying his true feelings. He hid how bad seasickness got to him because he didn't want to bother his dad.

He had a lot to reassess.

Sir Mallory tossed his cigar butt into the fire. "Well, my young friend, I have thoroughly enjoyed speaking with you, as always. You are one of the bright lights in this blizzard. Stay that way." He grinned at Will. "Now, let's try to get some sleep. We have another feeding in the morning."

"Okay. I do have a question, though."

His eyes widened. "Yes?"

"What's on the other side of the door with the keypad?"

"Oh, that. It's to the helicopter pad. I had that put in place just in case."

"In case of what?"

"Remember, I took every precaution." He smiled.

Will followed Sir Mallory up the stairs, watched him go into one of the first bedrooms, and spent about five minutes trying to remember which room was his. Finally, he decided to go to the one he'd hid in before. He knew right where that one was.

Once under the plush covers and in a T and sweatpants, he smiled. Ellen had known with her sisterly ways that he'd come back to this room and had brought his bag of clothes and toiletries here. Surprisingly, he fell asleep within minutes. Nothing like someone doing a thoughtful and psychic act like bringing you sweatpants to ease your mind so you can sleep, he thought as he drifted off, smiling slightly, sounds from the other side of the cave wall forgotten for the time being.

In the morning, he dressed and dashed down to the main hall. He didn't want to miss the feeding, and he was dying to see if the storm had cleared at all.

James gave him a salute, called him "young sailor Will," and told him the storm was still just as bad, if not worse. "You'll have to consult your dad on that one to be sure. He knows. I haven't seen him but through the monitors. He's in the enclosure with Sir Mallory, waiting for the sedative to wear all the way off before they feed. If you want to be there, you best hurry. Look." He pointed at the big monitor showing the enclosure from above. Will saw the gigantic white sharks doing their tight circles on opposite sides of the water, long, slender fins rising high toward the camera, just like they had before they'd rammed the walls. Yes, they were waking up and ready to eat or do some damage.

"Thanks, James," Will said, and ran all the way to the enclosure.

He was out of breath when he got there, but walked the last few steps and entered, hoping his father and Sir Mallory wouldn't know how he flew to get there, not wanting to miss a thing.

They were more toward the back wall, and all four of the green-suited men stood, two on each side of where the Megalodons swam, with their dart guns at the ready. Will joined his father and Sir Mallory. "Is it time to feed them?" he asked, trying to catch his breath without their noticing.

Sir Mallory grinned. "It is! We're herding the food through the food storage shoot as we speak."

"You enjoy watching them feed?" his father asked, eying him carefully.

"Yeah. It's cool."

"Blood doesn't bother you?" he asked.

"No. It's nature. I don't want it to happen to any more people, but seeing them feed is like…I dunno."

"Like what?" his father persisted.

Will thought carefully. "I guess it's seeing something no other person on Earth has ever seen before. Maybe."

His father nodded and was about to respond when suddenly, the Megalodons swam to the center of the water, spun, swung their tails and sped toward the back wall, slamming into it and shaking the entire enclosure. Will didn't lose his footing this time, even though none of them expected it, and neither did his father, Sir Mallory or the green-suited men.

"Sedate them," Will's father said as soon as they swam back to the center of the water, and made their fast circles there instead of at the edges of the walls.

Sir Mallory shook his head. "We have to feed them first. They will starve."

As he finished speaking, the Megalodons straightened up, swung their tails again, and rammed into the back of the cave, this time with more force. Will staggered and grabbed the wall behind him to keep from falling.

"Sedate them, now," Will's father commanded.

"The food should be ready." He signaled to the nearest green suit man. "Open the food gate, force them through."

Will's father left, and Will sensed his fury at Sir Mallory not listening to him. It irritated Will. Why couldn't his father chill out?

The giant sharks had gone back to the middle of the waters, now swimming in aggressive, frustrated circles, but suddenly stopped and sunk deep into the water with only the very tips of their dorsal fins poking out of the surface of the water.

The food must be out, Will thought, and his heartrate picked up.

He waited to see the shadows of large fish, but instead, a herd of fat snow seals swam to the surface in a frenzy, sticking close together and heading for the open sea blocked by steel bars.

The Megalodons instantly went into action.

The bigger of the two came at three of the smaller seals from the depths, snapping with teeth popping out upward at their bodies with its enormous maw, filling the enclosure with the stink of rotting death. It caught two right in its teeth, and the third was impaled by its thigh on a tooth. It squealed and red blood sprayed out over and under the water. The shark's eyes rolled back in its head, showing white, as though the taste of flesh and blood was true ecstasy. Will kept his mouth and nose covered with his shirt, but the smell still came through. There was so much blood, and that little white seal kept screaming and screaming as the Megalodon chewed the first two to pieces, leaving the impaled one for when these two were done. Will's stomach turned as it finished its first meal and then, eyes still white, began twisting its tongue around the third squealing snow seal, trying to get it in its mouth. Which it did. And the seal stopped its braying and instead exploded blood and flesh as the giant shark devoured it. Its eyes turned black again and it went on the hunt for more.

Meanwhile, the smaller Megalodon hunted, stalked, and then disabled about six white seals by biting them quickly at their midsections, but not hard enough to kill them. God, it was fast. Then, it fed on its prey one by one, but not before Will was subjected to wails of the dying, bleeding snow seals' pain.

More white seals could be seen in the now-red water of the enclosure, and the sharks fed, but the water was too murky to make out the devastation. There were more of the seals' desperate cries as the Megalodons finished them off.

Will's hands shook. Large fish were one thing, but seals were so…well, cute. It was like seeing puppies being massacred. He was both enthralled and horrified.

"Now," Sir Mallory said to a green-suited man, and the green suit man talked into his walkie-talkie.

The four of them shot darts into the Megalodons' gills as they shot out of the water for the last of the seals.

The larger one fought the sedative again, and Will swore it eyed the green-suited man who had gotten it as though marking him for a painful death for doing this.

Soon, the bloody waters settled and the sharks swam, sedated again, in lazy circles in the middle of the water around each other. One lone snow seal bobbed on the surface, one that had been a victim when the dart went into the larger's gills. It floated on its side with an enormous gash in its side, blood oozing out, from a giant, serrated tooth that hadn't gotten to finish the job.

Sir Mallory glanced at Will. "Kill the seal," he said. The green-suited man next to him pulled out a handgun and shot it dead in its head. It sunk below the red surface, never to be seen again.

Will and Sir Mallory were quiet for a time. "They are monsters," Sir Mallory said quietly.

Will didn't answer.

"Did you know," he continued, "that great white sharks are supposed to be ancestors of the Megalodons?"

"No."

"Yes, that is the theory. Of course, once we get word out about these, studies will be done to determine if that is so. Great whites are warm-blooded, as these Megalodons must be to survive in the Antarctic seas. Just look at them, Will." His voice was full of wonder, amazement now. "They are white, to blend in with the ice of these waters, to hunt without detection. If they were any other color, they'd have never survived. They wouldn't be able to sneak up on prey unless they blended like they do. They are too big. Prey would see them a mile away. But these? These are evolved. These are killing machines, apex predators of their time, and now perhaps our time, as well. Isn't it amazing?"

Will nodded slowly. "Yeah. Yeah, it is." He watched the blood washing down their white dorsal fins as they circled.

The nearby green-suited man said, "It's not working as long. Opposite of what we thought would happen."

Sir Mallory frowned, but said nothing.

Then Will heard it; they all did. Something on the other side of the back cave wall, scratching sounds. Almost like a chipmunk chewing through solid stone.

Sir Mallory turned to Will. "Is that the sound you and Captain Miller heard?" His voice was tight.

"Yeah." Will's voice didn't sound any more relaxed than Sir Mallory's.

The Englishman sighed and rubbed his forehead as the sound continued. "I'll have James run sonar scans of that area. It's nothing, I'm sure."

Will hoped he was right, but that nagging, gnawing doubt and fear ate at his stomach.

CHAPTER 12

Echoes of the snow seals' desperate death cries filled Will's mind, confusing him. It had been the first time he'd felt squeamish when the Megalodons fed from Sir Mallory's stock.

For the rest of the day, everyone went about their business, nobody really talking. Will found Ellen in the main hall at one point, and she tried to hide her unhappiness with their situation when she and Will talked, but he could sense it. He hated to see his sister like that.

It was around three in the afternoon when the sedative wore off, which was much sooner than it should have. They all knew it when James alerted them to the sharks' mad circling behavior they always had when the zombie dust wore off, and Sir Mallory gave the order to sedate them again at Will's father's insistence.

But it was too late. The Megalodons started slamming into the back cave wall again, according to the monitors, and everything shook and trembled.

Mallory madly barked into his walkie-talkie to the green-suited men, and Will heard their replies. "Not working...they built up tolerance...main defensive action..." was all he caught. He'd thought the zombie dust was supposed to kill them if they had too much, not that they could possibly build a tolerance. That gnawing pit of worry in his gut came up once more as the Megalodons smashed into the wall again and again, harder each time. All through the main hall, dishware and décor smashed to the marble floor, with shattering sounds that further gave Will's anxiety and feeling of foreboding a hard boost.

Everyone gathered in the main hall, except for the techies and the green-suited men. Don Mack wrung his hands as though they were cold, although the compound was warm as could be. He looked nervous. His father and Ellen were close to the fireplace, and Ellen looked terrified. Lady Katherine sat in her chair, and to Will, she seemed as detached as ever.

Will tried to hear more of the walkie-talkie exchange between Sir Mallory and the green-suited men, but Sir Mallory had gone far from the others and spoke in hushed tones. The messages back were so full of static that Will made out nothing but the panicked tones of their voices.

Trepidation and tension filled the hall each time the sharks hammered the cave wall. The very foundation of the compound might crack under this stress, Will thought. Even as the idea crossed his mind, he ran to the techies' room and watched on the monitors as the Megalodons slammed the back cave wall more and more frantically. They looked bigger than usual on the screens, but then suddenly, they stopped and swam to the front of the enclosure by the steel bars…as though waiting for something…

Then all hell broke loose.

And Will saw the beginnings of it onscreen.

The back wall of the giant cave enclosure, which was supposed to have been full of steel bars, burst into pieces. Chunks of solid rock and steel flew through the air, and one knocked out a camera. Something was coming through that back wall, breaking through with impossible strength, and it was big…bigger than the two Megalodons.

The compound shuddered like its walls, too, might crumble from the impact. Will heard screams, but kept his eyes and mind focused on the monitors. He heard Ellen and his dad calling out for him.

As the dust cleared from the broken enclosure's inner wall, Will made out a gigantic, long white fin, much bigger than the Megalodons' fins, rising out of the enclosure water and nearly scraping the ceiling.

"Jesus," James hissed. "Jesus, Jesus, Jesus Christ! It's another one, and it's fucking huge!"

There was still too much dust in the air and murk in the water to make out what lie beneath the surface, but Will knew James was right. Will's hands shook and sweated.

The fin rested in the back, middle of the enclosure, and two smaller white dorsal fins hovered on either side of it, facing the open air blocked by steel bars. If that new Megalodon could smash through the cave wall, Will had no doubt that it could get through those bars with enough effort.

Just then, the trio of prehistoric gargantuan predator sharks made a rush at the steel bars, the big one in front.

The monitors went black just as the wall between the compound and the enclosure burst into pieces. An enormous, white fin slashed through the wall, going so fast and wreaking so much havoc that Will couldn't process it. One of the crewmen's head got chopped clear in half by the thing, blood spurting from his neck as his headless body fell. His head flew off, unseen by Will ever again.

The fin ripped the eastern side of the compound to pieces and everything began falling apart. Will had spun around from the tech room in time to see it all. God, it was huge. And the crewman…oh, God.

Will realized he was on the floor. Had he fallen, or had the impact knocked him off his feet? He wasn't sure, couldn't remember. It was all happening so fast.

The fin sliced clear through, and the front of the compound, which had no outer door, fell to pieces as the new Megalodon rammed against the steel bars over and over, its white fin moving back and forth in the compound's main hall with each effort, further breaking down the foundation of their haven.

Freezing air hit Will in the face, and the blizzard, which they'd been safe and warm from, now took over everything inside. More screams as the giant Megalodon's fin sliced through the front of the compound with an especially forceful push at the steel bars, and Will knew it had escaped, taking the other two with it.

"Out!" yelled Don Mack. "We all gotta get out!"

Will couldn't distinguish who was who in the dust and mess hanging in the air and filling the compound. He heard more voices screaming the same thing as Don Mack, and he shook himself out of his daze. He got up and ran, ran to the now-open front of the compound and out into the white wall of the blizzard.

He was wearing casual clothes, nothing to protect him from the deadly cold elements, but once outside, he felt hot with fear and tension. In the swirling snow, he saw figures dashing about. He heard his father calling his name. The ocean was merely twenty feet from the compound, and through the white storm, Will saw something even whiter. Three fins, with the one in the middle rising up thirty feet from the sea, all pointed at them. At him, it felt.

Then they attacked the short beach, and the massive Megalodon charged first, followed by the smaller ones they'd held in captivity. It ran itself up on shore, body still in the water, and through the storm, Will saw its head, resting on the beach, open its mouth. Its teeth popped out in that unnerving way right before eating, and it scooped up three human figures off the ground, black eyes rolling back in its head and turning white. The most rank smell ever hit Will, and he saw red blood squirt out across the snow-covered shore, and wails burned Will's ears. The giant shark's face was splattered with crimson human blood. Whoever those people were, they were being eaten alive in open air. This monster didn't care that it couldn't breathe at the moment. It had revenge on its demonic mind.

What if any of those people were his sister and father?

Will got as far from the shoreline as possible, gaping now at just how huge this new Megalodon was. It had to be thirty feet bigger than the other two, judging by the size of its head, which now withdrew back to the sea for a breather.

The crowd of people left all backed off the shoreline, having seen what happened, too, but even as many of them joined Will, the compound began crumbling in on itself, the structure completely devastated. Chunks of the building fell all around them, and Will ran to the west, where the ship's dock was. If his father and sister were anywhere, that's where they'd be.

He stumbled almost blindly through the steely snow stinging his flesh, and through the swirling, freezing snow, he saw others heading toward the ship, too, nearby him. There was no communicating. No yelling at the top of his lungs to get anyone's attention. The thundering sounds of the compound collapsing made that impossible.

Will heard more screams just before he reached the haven of the ship's port, and glanced back, not wanting to, but having to see…see what was happening, who was dying.

The big Megalodon had risen up on the beach again, just its head, and the wind shifted a tad so that the snowstorm allowed him a clearer view.

Lady Katherine stood before the huge thing, stoic and seemingly unafraid. She fell to her knees just as the Megalodon's teeth popped out at her, taking her into its giant mouth, and she squealed and shrieked as the serrated teeth crunched her frail body into minced meat. Her blood flew through the air and splattered the now-blood-soaked shore, as well as the Megalodon's face. Her screams stopped short, and Will saw that her head had been severed and was impaled on one of the Megalodon's front, sharp, giant teeth. Her facial features had distorted from being spiked, and her blonde hair was soaked red with blood. Her eyes had popped out of their sockets and hung on tendons, dangling on her cheeks. Her mouth fell open forever in an unfinished wail of pain and horror.

"No!" Will heard Sir Mallory cry out. Will made out his form nearby where Lady Katherine had been, and Sir Mallory pulled out a handgun and began shooting at the shark's face, screaming curses and crying. The Megalodon retreated quickly, and all three fins went under water.

"Sir Mallory!" Will called to him. "You have to come with us. Come with us to the ship!"

"My Katty!" He fell to the snow and put his head in his hands. Will ran to him, despite fears that the giant Megalodon might come back at any moment, and pulled him up to his feet. His face was red with fury, eyes streaming tears of anger and anguished loss.

"Don't think, just come with me!"

"I can't leave her!"

"She's gone! Now you have to come, have to come to the ship. We have to get out of here before it comes back. Before they all come back. Come on!" Will encouraged.

Sir Mallory numbly let Will lead him away from the shore and to the ship's port to the west. Will hoped the now-crushed compound's devastation hadn't affected the ship's dock. Now, he felt the cold as his clothes became soaked through and the pause in the storm that had allowed him to see Lady Katherine's demise was gone. The blizzard raged harder than ever, as though reflecting Sir

Mallory's devastation at losing his beloved wife in a most horrible way.

Somehow, Will got himself and Sir Mallory to the ship's port in the blinding white. The rank smell from the giant Megalodon's breath still hung in the air, but Will was in too much of a rush to get away to be too bothered by it.

Once in the shelter of the dock, Will saw the ship was intact and most of the crew and Sir Mallory's people were there.

"Will!" Ellen came running from the crowd, short hair and clothes soaked. She grabbed him in her arms and hugged him as though she'd never let go. Finally, she pulled back and said, "Come on, Dad's worried to death about you." She tugged his hand toward the boat.

"Sir Mallory?" Will said, turning to him, but he wasn't there. Worry hit him yet again, but he decided to go with Ellen. She led him through the frantic, freezing crowd to their father, who, upon laying eyes on Will, let his tight shoulders sag in relief.

"I found him. He's alright, Dad." Ellen hugged Will again.

"Thank God," was all his father said, and then he turned to the frenzied and terrified people all around them. "We have to get back onboard. We have to sail out of here while they are submerged. They're north of us, so we'll sail west, around them, then to the coast of Argentina. I've sent out distress calls, but with this weather..."

Everyone listened, but the general level of hope that they'd escape this nightmare felt at the lowest of the lows.

Sir Mallory appeared next to Will's father. "No, no. We can't leave. My wife...and we haven't documented...and...and..."

Will's father glared at him. "Do you think we can survive this storm without shelter?"

"We can take shelter on the boat, just stay here, just stay here," he answered.

"I'm afraid to get on the ship again," said one of Nancy's girls. "They'll come after us, I just know they will. I can't see any more of this. We'll all die!"

"We'll all die here even if we take shelter on the ship and stay," said Will's father. "Those monsters will find us here. That big one, I'd bet she's their mother. She has to be sixty, seventy feet long.

And they swarm her like children. They will come here, and then we will all die."

Silence.

"I agree with Captain Miller," said Don Mack. His black hair was a wild, wet, and snow-covered mess. He hadn't been wearing his usual sailing hat since they'd first arrived. "We're safer at sea where we can navigate away. Captain knows how to sail these waters, you all know it. He'll get us away from the sharks."

"No," said Sir Mallory, his voice stronger now. "No, we have to stand here and fight. We can't fight them on a boat. They have the advantage in the water."

"Fight?" Will's father barked. "Fight with what?"

"You saw how the big one came right up on shore. Not safe here. And the weather will kill us if the sharks don't. Come on, man," said Don Mack.

Sir Mallory straightened up and looked around. "Who is missing, other than my wife?"

"Two crew members and Ken," answered James. Ken was one of the techies Will hadn't gotten a chance to know. Those must've been the three he saw the mother Megalodon get onshore first.

Sir Mallory looked down and ran a hand through wet, snow-covered hair. "What do all of you think? Do you agree with the captain?"

Nobody said anything, not wanting to make the wrong decision or not being able to decide. Fear ran like electricity through their whole group.

"We go," said Will's father. "We go now. We go directly west and I'll know when to start north. Hell, we might even sail out of this blizzard."

"Can you navigate this storm?" Sir Mallory asked.

"Oh, yes." Will's father met eyes with Sir Mallory for a long time. "I'm sorry about your wife," he added softly.

Sir Mallory's mouth tightened, and then he said, "Okay, we sail. We sail."

"What about the helicopter?" Will asked.

Sir Mallory shook his head. "It must be buried with the remnants of the compound. Besides, no flying it in this weather. So yes, we sail."

CHAPTER 13

Will threw up over the railing within ten minutes of sailing on the incredibly rough and stormy sea. He wasn't the only one, so at least there was that.

He was scared. Actually scared for real for the first time on the trip. What was going to happen to them? Would they be rescued? Would the Megalodons come back for them? Did his dad really know what he was doing? He hoped so.

Tension filled the ship. Most people had come from below deck after changing clothes, drying off and putting on parkas. Nobody's stomachs could stay stable in the cabins. The ship rocked and bobbed like it was a toy boat in a two-year-old's bathtub. The blizzard was so thick that the late afternoon sunlight had filtered to near-darkness. Never had Will felt cold like this.

Ellen hadn't left Will's side except when they changed clothes. Their father and Don Mack were busy on the bridge, so that's where Ellen and Will went. Will had to keep swallowing vomit every few minutes, but that was the least of his worries. After seeing what happened to Lady Katherine, he was grateful he was still alive to feel seasick.

The sailors didn't notice Will and Ellen. They worked like a smooth and comfortable team, yelling back and forth to each other to be heard. His father had steering, black whip swinging madly at his hip, and Don Mack was watching the waters ahead, giving warnings to Will's dad if he saw ice, and intermittently screaming into a radio that answered back with nothing but static. His black hair stood out everywhere, and his nose was as red as it ever had been.

"Willie, maybe we should go on deck," Ellen said to him in a low voice.

"Why?" Will choked out, swallowing another bit of bile.

"Because you're turning green. Let's go."

He didn't argue. The cold would be a blessing if it stopped his stomach upheaval.

On deck, Sir Mallory's people had opened up the one mysterious giant crate that had been left on the boat, the crate that Will had wondered about what felt like years ago. They pulled huge guns, missile launchers, grenades out. Ellen grabbed Will's arm, mouth open, pointing at them. "Would you look at that? Dad's gonna be pissed."

"What? What do you mean?" Will felt relief at seeing the crew also take up arms. Even though the storm made visibility low, Will could make out the immediate happenings on deck around them.

"He hates weapons. Guns. You know that. Now, anyway." She shielded her brown eyes from a particularly fierce blast of wind and sleet, as did Will.

He wanted to say more, but had to run to the rail and puke. Ellen followed, patting his back as he got the last of the food in his belly out and dry heaved until he couldn't breathe.

"It's okay, it's okay," Ellen soothed.

By the time Will had his bearings again, he heard Sir Mallory over the wind and waves. He was giving instructions on where to stand on the boat, what to do with the weapons. People surrounded the edges of every part of the ship, loaded with massive amounts of firepower.

Then it occurred to Will. Would these measly guns and grenades be enough for three Megalodons if they came after the ship? What if there were more Megalodons in the sea? There had to be. If the huge one was the mother, then they bred here, and that meant there could be countless numbers of the giant monsters. He felt colder at the thought, if that were possible.

Suddenly, Will heard his father's screaming from the bridge. He'd opened a window up there and yelled at Sir Mallory. "You brought *those* on my ship without telling me? What the fuck? You'll get us all killed!"

Sir Mallory ignored Will's father, still giving frantic instructions. His cheeks were more sunken than before, eyes wild with grief and madness. All he yelled back to Will's father was, "We have to finish this! For her, for us all!"

Will's father yelled something back, but the words were lost in a gale. The tone of his voice wasn't, however. He was, as Ellen said, pissed. Next, Will made out his father calling for him and Ellen.

They made their way back to the bridge, stumbling, and Will dry heaved one more time on the stairs to the bridge.

Once there, Don Mack had the wheel, and their father's eyes were oddly steady and hard. Will realized his dad was in a zone, operating on instinct and awareness. He knew then that his dad had been in a situation like this before at some point in his life, and he wanted to know about it. But now wasn't the time.

Their father touched both their shoulders. "I'm so sorry," he said, looking at each of them directly in the eyes, conveying deepest regrets. "I never should have brought you on this expedition. I don't know what I was thinking. It was that…it was that…" He lost his words but continued to stare hard at them. "We'll get through this."

"It's almost night, Dad," Ellen said. "We won't be able to see them coming if they do."

All he said was, "I'm so sorry, I'm so sorry."

"Captain, get back here!" Don Mack screamed, breaking the moment. "I can't navigate this alone. Come on! You kids, get back!"

Their father got back to steering, and still, the radio sizzled static like the world was gone, and the people on their little ship in the Antarctic sea were the only humans left on the planet. It was as though they'd gone back in time, back to the age of dinosaurs and apex predators more deadly than any that came after them. They were stuck, people were dead, and soon, they all might be, too.

Night was coming, and fast.

CHAPTER 14

The darkness the blizzard had enveloped the ship in had already blackened the sky, so when night came, it was as though sunlight had never been. They'd skipped a day.

Will stayed on deck watching the crew, the three remaining green-suited men, and who was left of Mallory's team hold the ship with massive firepower ready to go.

Tension was as thick as the storm. Will felt afraid. He always was vulnerable at sea, but now, fear settled his stomach, oddly enough. Either that, or he had finally gotten his sea legs right when he needed them most. He doubted that was the case.

It was pure, ice-cold fear that the gigantic sharks were coming, coming after them this night, waiting until they slipped, weren't looking. Then they would all come with their serrated teeth ready to shred and devour more human flesh. His family's flesh…his own.

He had the hood of his parka tight over his head to block the icy wind and sleet, but he didn't feel as cold as he should, and his heart pounded relentlessly in anticipation of what was to come that night.

Will felt as though he had some understanding of the Megalodons that the others didn't have. He couldn't explain it, but maybe it was from spending so much time in the enclosure. Or maybe it went back to the time in Nancy's tent when he watched the first babe swimming behind the ship so many eons ago. He knew, just *knew*, they'd come, and soon.

He was right.

In the blackness of the blizzard-filled night on the roughest seas Will had known, he watched over the railing with his sister at his side, and for once, his arm was around her as she shivered and shook from the freezing cold. Darkness looked back, but then, in the light of the ship's portholes and deck lamps, he saw them: three slender, white fins, one towering over the other two, simply seeming to hover in space in the distance of nothingness itself. He knew nobody had seen them yet but him, and he wanted to call out to warn everyone, but when he did, his voice froze.

They weren't circling. They waited, assessing their attack. Was this ship something dangerous to them? Were these tasty, fleshy things going to hurt them some more? Oh no, they weren't, not if the sharks had anything to say about it.

Then, Ellen saw them, too, and she let out a shriek.

Instantly, the ship exploded into action as the fins drew closer. Will first heard machine gun fire, and then as the ship bobbed on the rough water, the fins appeared, disappeared, and then reappeared. He couldn't see if the now three machine guns were doing any damage to the Megalodons, but he knew he had to get Ellen to the other side of the ship before any or all of them made a slamming rush at the boat.

He grabbed her hand and tugged. She was stuck to her spot, frozen by cold and fear. "Come on, Ellen, we have to get to the other side of the ship. Come on!" He pulled harder.

She broke out of her trance, yanked her hand out of his, and covered her ears with her hands. Of course, she couldn't have heard him over the gunshots, but she had to know what he meant. She closed her eyes tightly and started to hunch over in a ball.

"No!" Will yelled, and pulled her up by the armpits. He dragged her across the deck in a sliding, wet rush through the sleeting storm. The gunfire continued, and he glanced back midway to the other side of the boat in time to see one of the smaller fins have a bullet rip through the tip. Black blood in the night squirted out, and the fin instantly submerged.

The big fin, however, would not stand for this. It kept coming, faster now, and a spread of firepower crossed the middle of it. The white fin was spotted black now, but on it came, even faster. Nothing could stop this beast.

Will got Ellen to the other side of the ship just as the mother of the Megalodons rammed the ship. Both he and Ellen fell on their sides, and rolled into the railing posts as the ship bowed to the side, but his father knew what he was doing; the ship straightened up as much as it could in the storm almost as quickly as it had rocked to the side from the enormous fish's slam. More gunfire, and then as the ship was as steady as could be hoped for, the third Megalodon made a charge and banged against the side.

Will and Ellen were still down, and again the boat tilted to the side, but not all the way over like with the big one. Still, Ellen rolled out of Will's grasp and over the edge of the ship, her fingertips showing at the rim of the deck's floor.

Will grasped for her hands, thinking of Caleb as he heard grenades going off behind him. The ship rolled up, and Will pulled his screaming sister up and back onto the deck. Her hood had fallen back, and her short, brown hair was wet, stuck all over her face and head. Her wide eyes held a panic prisoner, but as she caught her breath and realized she hadn't gone overboard, she grabbed Will in a hug. He felt her screaming something, but he couldn't make out what it was as another grenade went off behind him.

The scent hit.

One of the three, or maybe all of them, had a mouth open. That meant there was a vulnerable target and the monster knew it, and planned fully to exploit it right away. Will whipped his head around in time to see a green-suited man and two crewmen firing machine guns at an enormous, gaping, sharp-toothed mouth heading right for one of Nancy's girls at the front of the ship. She was one of the grenade-tossing people, and one of the few who hadn't been tossed clear across the ship, and she held a grenade out as the mouth of the smallest Megalodon came rushing at her. The boat tilted in the shark's favor for a nice snack.

She hurled the grenade, but it was too late, and her panicked aim too far off. As the grenade exploded underwater, the Megalodon's teeth popped out toward the poor girl, and even as the machine guns took chunks out of the huge shark's cheek, its eyes rolled back, showing white. It bit down on the top half of her body and slipped back into the sea with her, leaving a huge splash of blood and seawater in her place, along with that horrid scent Will knew was decomposing body parts in its belly.

Now she was becoming one of those bodies, and the gunfire stopped momentarily as the shooters were stunned by what they had seen and what they now heard of her screams of pain and terror.

Will couldn't see her, but after Lady Katherine, he didn't think he could see much worse. Another victim claimed, and just then, the big Megalodon rammed the ship again. Will fell back onto Ellen, and they both slid into a rail post as the ship rocked to the side and skipped over the icy sea. Ellen grabbed Will around his neck in a panic, but the rail post kept them steady—or maybe it was because Will had them both wrapped in a death-grip around it as the ship cruised harshly across the violent ocean.

Don Mack's voice carried with command over them all as the gunshots stopped from the big shark's stunning hit. She'd attacked with even more force this time. Will couldn't make out what the first mate wanted them to know.

Why weren't she and the other, bigger baby Megalodon trying to eat people like the brave, smallest yet giant shark? Will figured they must be put off by the firepower.

The boat straightened, and Will and Ellen jumped to their feet. Guns went off again, and Will grabbed Ellen by her shoulders, screaming into her ear to be heard. "Go to the bridge. Go!"

"No!" she yelled back. "We stick together. You're not leaving my side! Come with me."

"Go!" he hollered, shoving her in the direction of the stairwell.

She glared at him, and grabbed his upper arms in both her hands. "No! Come with me!"

"I'm getting a gun."

"No."

He pulled her hand and dragged her as she wailed protests. The sea heaved them up and down, and as they got closer to the bridge's stairwell, Will saw the fins again. The damaged fin, which belonged to the bigger of the two baby Megalodons, was ripped to shreds by the gunfire, and all three fins now circled madly at the port side just beyond reach of their hungry mouths' aching grips. They'd gotten smart about staying in one place; they'd figured out the guns didn't hit them as much or often if they were on the move.

Another grenade went off in the water amidst the sharks' mad circling, lighting up the water for a moment as Will shoved Ellen roughly up the stairs. She started to turn on him and fight, but then the smell that lingered refreshed anew. A mouth had opened, and Ellen saw it. She froze in place on the stairs, mouth gaping as she stared at the green-suited man.

Will looked behind them, prepared for the worst. He was not disappointed.

The bigger Megalodon baby, whose now-deformed dorsal fin Will had just taken note of, had decided to take on the guns, unafraid—or simply it had been chosen to test for weakness. Maybe because it was already so damaged.

Its teeth gleamed in the ship's lights, and Will could make out those sharp spikes on its gigantic teeth as they popped out at the green-suited man. He unloaded his machine gun into its mouth as it snapped him in half, blood from both the green suit man and the shark's gullet gushing out as the mouth clamped closed. The Megalodon opened its mouth again to chew as it sunk into the water, and some of its teeth were missing. The green-suited man was still alive in there, but bent in half at the waist. Will saw him, and for the first time, he seemed like something more than a green-suited man. He was a human whose body was being crushed and ripped apart by giant, prehistoric shark teeth in rolling, bloody, stinking bites. He had a family, maybe. Kids. A wife.

He kept firing, but Will could tell it wasn't out of bravery or fight. His face was white and blank with pain and horror, and his aim was sporadic. Bullets flew back at the ship, and one took out a crewman shooting a gun nearby. Bullet went right through his skull, spraying brain matter out the back and across the deck.

The smaller Megalodon snapped his fallen body up by the feet like a snake striking a pet store mouse, snagging the man's body into the frigid, swirling sea.

God, the smell. Will felt bile rise up in his throat for the first time since his fear hit him, but it wasn't seasickness. It was that awful stench. Rotting flesh, once only fish and seal bodies, but now, humans disintegrated in their stomachs, too.

"Ellen, go!" Will yelled, even though no guns fired at the moment. Most of the people who'd been fighting on that side of the ship had been thrown to the other side, or overboard, when they'd been rammed by the Megalodons. The remaining had been eaten, except for a crewman and one green-suited man. They seemed too stunned to fire, and the crewman vomited all over the front of his parka. The puke froze instantly.

Ellen looked at him desperately, and then said, "You be careful, and you don't die or Dad will kill me." She kissed his cheek and dashed up the stairs, running through the bridge door and slamming it.

Will was alone with the two men, who had gotten their acts together and were launching grenades into the water. A third guy, one of the techies Will had seen in the monitor room, came up next to them with a missile launcher, but he couldn't manage it by himself on the rough seas while handling the nerves of trying to fight three giant sharks from before time began.

That's where Will would start.

He ran to the man's aid, sliding on his knees for the last few steps as the ship churned, and grabbed the base of the weapon.

The man yelled back to him, "Thanks, mate!" and aimed the huge gun at all three of the circling fins. Grenades went off around the sharks, and they lit up the giant fish figures in bloody silhouette. One hit the smallest Megalodon in its tail, blowing it off. Pieces of bloody shark tail flew through the air as the techie, being a smart guy, aimed at the now-disabled and floundering Megalodon, and launched a missile right at its side as it struggled to swim straight without a tail fin.

The missile landed square, exploding sound hitting Will's ears as shark blood and flesh landed on his bare face, freezing there. Before he closed his eyes in reflex, he saw a huge hole in the Megalodon, which was now floating on one side, unmoving.

Will heard Sir Mallory for the first time. He hadn't seen the man since it all started. He couldn't make out what Sir Mallory screamed, but he seemed to be cheering. Will looked behind him and saw Sir Mallory running to his side of the deck. Blood oozed from the shoulder of his parka. He must've been hit by a bullet in the fray.

He reached Will and the techie, and clapped their shoulders. Then he pulled out a huge machine gun from the back of his waistband. It had been tucked away under his coat. The man knew how to fight. He'd been rocked by the sharks' slamming into the ship, and hit by a bullet, but still had the sense to keep his weapon safe and handy while it all happened.

More gunfire and grenades went off, but the two remaining Megalodons had fallen back when the smallest was obliterated.

"Fantastic…Will, you are a trooper…we have to get them all! Recharge!" Sir Mallory's voice carried between bursts of guns and explosions.

Sir Mallory took Will's place, handing him the machine gun. Will lost his footing as he stood, and Sir Mallory caught him before he fell on his face.

"Just pull the trigger," he yelled to Will, demonstrating what to do by putting his hands around the huge gun, and then turning away.

Of course, Will had never fired any gun—with the exception of just having been half of a two-man team to use a rocket launcher to kill a giant shark—but he'd seen the movies. There was recoil, there was aim, there was loud sound.

Will got next to a green-suited man as another joined them, and aimed the gun out to sea. Two fins circled like angry bees around an intruder to their nest. They were barely visible in the blizzard; the lights from the ship didn't reach as far out as they'd gone to reassess their attack.

It didn't take them long.

As Sir Mallory and the crewman reloaded the missile launcher, the baby Megalodon who was left made a rush at the ship.

Except for the last time the boat was rammed, they'd seemingly been holding back, but this time, the Megalodon came full-force, with water spraying out behind it. Will suddenly saw what his father had talked about. The shark had its nose pointed down just as it reached the side of the ship and, amidst the explosions of the fighting men, with some of its white flesh getting chunks taken out and leaving bloody trails, it hit.

The lights of the ship flickered off and on with the impact. This time, Will flew off his feet, clinging to the machine gun, and careened backward through the air. He didn't have time to panic or be afraid, just react on gut instinct. The sound of gunfire stopped as the others, too, had been knocked back.

He landed against the base of the bridge, first hitting the wall, and then sliding down to sitting position with his feet straight out in front of him. The wind was knocked out of him and he gasped for a breath of freezing air. The back of his head banged against the metal, stunning his field of vision for a moment. He felt the boat skimming on the surface of the water, that skipping stone sensation, and heard his father yelling something to Don Mack.

Suddenly, the ship whacked into something in the water and stopped dead, flipping upright at the same time.

Will whipped his head around and crawled out of his spot to look at what had stopped the boat.

He saw a huge chunk of solid white in madly swirling white in the lights of the boat. They'd hit ice, and it seemed they were stranded on it.

He worried that the boat had been compromised, that the hull might have been punctured and they'd all sink soon, but even as the thought passed, he heard his father call out over the ship's speakers, "All safe! Ship intact, I repeat, ship intact! Continue on!"

He saw people all around the deck getting up and gaining balance, and then running to the port side to do as Will's father said. Fight with guns drawn.

Sir Mallory and the crewman had lost the missile launcher in the attack, but they'd both found other guns, probably had them on them. Sir Mallory only had a handgun, but he was gathering grenades from a green suit man. Will got a hard grip on the machine gun and, swallowing his fear, got up and made a slippery, mad dash for the edge of the boat where the two remaining sharks must be planning their next moves.

Once at the rail, Will saw that the two Megalodons had moved back again, circling fins dancing just out of reach. Guns flared, and Will wanted to join the fight. He held up the machine gun with the butt end against his shoulder like he saw others doing, put his right pointer on the trigger, aimed at the smaller of the two Megalodon fins, took a deep, cold breath, and squeezed the trigger.

The kickback was no joke, and Will's gunfire sprayed straight at first, but he lost control of his gun and soon, the bullets flew into the sky as he fell onto the deck, releasing the trigger just in time to not shoot any people.

The first thought he had was to wonder if he'd landed any hits to the shark, but then someone was pulling him up from his armpits and yanking the weapon from his hands.

"No, you don't fight!" It was his father. "You go to the bridge, now," he yelled over the gunfire.

He must have seen Will and run down here.

"I have to fight!" he argued, getting his footing and grabbing at the gun in his father's hands.

"Will, I mean it."

"Dad, you have to let me. I can do this."

"You almost killed people. You can't use a gun, and not one of these for sure."

Will grabbed his father's neck and screamed into his ear. "Get back to taking care of the ship. I got this."

His father's dark eyes looked hollowly back at him. "We're dead in the water, stuck on ice."

Will glanced back at the imposing chunk of frozen water they'd been forced upon, then back at his father. "Then we fight together," he said.

His dad's eyes narrowed for a moment, thinking, and then he took Will's arm and led him at a run to Sir Mallory.

"Give him grenades. Give Will grenades, Mallory."

Sir Mallory had just tossed one, which exploded near a fin in the air, doing no damage. He turned, wild-eyed, saying, "Here, here." He pulled four grenades out of the pockets of his parka and handed them to Will.

His dad demonstrated how to use the grenade, mimicking pulling the pin and throwing. "Got it? Don't be a hero."

"Got it. I won't."

His dad turned to the rail, braced his elbows on it with the gun propped in aiming position, and began to fire. Will saw the smaller Megalodon's thin, white fin instantly explode at the top, gushing black blood like a geyser. No longer coming to a point, the fin submerged in retreat.

Sir Mallory hurled a grenade to where the shark had just been, and Will took note and pulled the pin on a grenade in his hand. The other three he'd tucked into his pockets.

"Throw it!" Sir Mallory beckoned him.

He chucked it hard toward where he'd last seen the fin, but the Megalodon was surfacing right in front of them, its white face spotted with bullet holes, its mouth opening with a most putrid smell. Will's grenade went off underwater behind it, but he hardly noticed as the shark's teeth, some missing from its maw, popped out at Sir Mallory, his father and the green-suited man fighting there.

"No!" Will screamed, imaginings flashing through his head of his father being devoured alive by the beast like he'd seen so many be massacred.

Its bottom teeth got stuck on the ship's metal, but the top half of its mouth clamped down on the green-suited man, front teeth sawing him completely in half from the top of his head to his crotch. The man didn't even have time to scream, and Will hoped he also didn't have time to realize what was happening to him. The man's innards spilled out all over the deck, and his face landed in a pile of blood and guts. His eye sockets were empty voids, the eyeballs having been forced out of his skull. They rolled away from the man's body parts as the ship careened with the shark attack's force.

The Megalodon struggled to free itself from the ship, but its teeth were locked on tightly. It shook its head from side to side, blood flying all over the deck, the green-suited man's body parts taking to the air and landing around the remaining fighters. The boat rocked, but the ice held it firmly in place from the madly frustrated Megalodon.

His father made a rush at the shark's open front teeth, knelt right in front of a missing tooth, inches from the Megalodon's nose, and emptied the machine gun into the gap. Sir Mallory joined him, chucking a grenade in the tooth hole, too.

Will's father yelled angrily at Sir Mallory as the grenade went off.

All at once, the giant shark's head exploded with the sound stinging Will's ears. Shark brains, flesh, and blood sprayed all over him and the others, and the Megalodon's lifeless, headless body sunk into the sea, leaving its bloody teeth still clamped to the deck and hull. A part of its face was still attached to the teeth, and one black eye seemed to turn and look at Will dead-on, and then it rolled back, turning white.

Will's father had a reason for chastising Sir Mallory. The ship's hull had taken damage from the grenade that had been tossed so close to it. The railing where the top teeth were stuck and parts of the green-suited man's body still lay was blown out, and Will could see through the teeth out to sea, where the mama Megalodon's fin had stopped circling and now sunk into the water.

Was the hull under the water damaged? Will felt the vibrations of the deck under his feet, surprised he had this instinct. No, the ship would be okay for now, he could tell.

The guns quieted.

Will looked around. There was blood everywhere, shark and human. Pieces of both clung to the deck and walls of the ship, too. There were so few people left and it sickened Will.

His father turned to him, walked over, and clapped him on the shoulder, giving him a hard look that Will couldn't interpret. He looked younger, eyes wild and fierce. "Now, go to the bridge, tell Don Mack to announce that we need to get off this iceberg. Whoever is left needs to help."

Will stared at him.

"Go on, go! The big one isn't coming back tonight."

"How do you know?"

"I just do. Go." He turned away and dashed below deck, and Will assumed he was checking the damage with his own eyes.

He turned and ran to the bridge stairwell, up the stairs, and onto the bridge to do his father's bidding.

CHAPTER 15

Not many people were left, but of those who were, they were able to rescue James off the ice. He'd flown out there when the little Megalodon hit the hardest time, and nobody had noticed. When everything had died down, he'd called out and the four remaining crewmen had pulled him aboard with ropes.

The whole ship was covered in blood, pieces of flesh, and guts. Will's father, Don Mack, and the crewmen worked to get the ship off the ice throughout the night, and Sir Mallory, the two remaining green-suited men, James, and the techie Will had shot the rocket launcher with kept watch for the massive Megalodon still out there somewhere. All Nancy's girls were gone, as were the rest of the tech crew.

Will and Ellen stayed on the bridge where it was somewhat warm. Will didn't need an open window; his stomach still felt steady. Ellen didn't say much, and halfway through the long night, she fell asleep.

Will thought he'd never sleep again.

The sun rose, and the blizzard died off enough to show where the shining star was in the sky on the horizon through the clouds. Gales of forty to fifty miles an hour rocked the ship as, at daybreak, the crew was successful in detaching the boat from the iceberg. Will's father and Don Mack were on the bridge in a flash.

"Is everything okay?" Will asked them right away.

His father nodded as Don Mack said, "Little bit of damage to the hull, but we're not taking on water."

Sir Mallory entered the bridge then, looking pale and frail, but wild-eyed and fiery at the same time. "It didn't come back. It didn't come back."

"Good," Will's father said, seeming to appease Sir Mallory as he sunk into a chair near a window.

"Never thought we'd see sunlight again there for a minute," Don Mack said.

Sir Mallory's hair was matted with frozen red blood, and his face was streaked with it. He had a piece of someone or something's flesh stuck in his eyebrow. "Have you reached anyone on the radio?"

"No," Will's father said. "Static. But we've called out all night, and had the distress signal out since we left port. Now, we sail north."

"North? That's right through their territory!" Sir Mallory said.

"No," Will's father said. "We don't know where their territory is, exactly. We just have *her* to deal with. She'll be back, she's still around. We have to go north, straight to Argentina, as fast as we can move."

"We should go east, then north," Sir Mallory replied.

"No. That'll take too long in case our radio signals never got caught. Someone would be here by now if they had, most likely. Listen." His father turned up the radio. Sizzling airwaves came back at them.

Sir Mallory slowly nodded. "You know best, Captain Miller. I trust you."

Will's dad gave the Englishman an indescribable look, and then turned to the controls of the ship. "Will, help Mallory and his people watch the sea. Warn us of anything, and tell the others the same."

Will hopped up. Was his dad including him like an equal? He had to make sure he did a good job if that was the case.

As if he wouldn't either way. A seventy-foot-long Megalodon was most likely hunting them now. He was tired of sitting on the bridge feeling useless and helpless. "Thanks, Dad," he said, and joined Sir Mallory. He glanced back as they left, and his father was watching him with a curiously dark expression.

"Come with me, Will," Sir Mallory said. His shoulder had been cleaned and bandaged in the night, but he still favored it, not moving his left arm much.

Will followed him to the deck and over to the crate that had held the massive store of weapons that had saved their lives the night before. "We don't have much left," Sir Mallory said as he opened it and leaned inside. "One rocket launcher, three machine guns, and six grenades. We have to make these count if she comes back." His eyes were steely bright and his voice held excitement.

Will paused as Sir Mallory handed him three of the grenades, simply holding the destructive metal cylinders dumbly. "You want it to, don't you?"

He stopped awkwardly unloading the missile launcher and turned to Will. The wild look wasn't gone, but he did seem sad. "No, and yes, to be honest. But not for the reasons you think."

"You haven't proved it to the world yet, though," Will said to him. "You had one life goal, and that was to catch a Megalodon. You still want to?"

He shook his head and looked down, and then rubbed his face with his right hand. "No, no. I would say you couldn't understand, but you can. I know you can." He looked back up at Will, some of the maddened light leaving his eyes. "It's about Katty. She took her from me," he said in a low tone. "Took her, destroyed her into pieces." His voice broke at the end and he looked down again.

Will paused, not knowing what to say, and then pocketed the grenades in his parka. "I'm sorry," was all he came up with.

Sir Mallory looked out to sea as the ship gained speed, heading due north. "Hard to explain. Perhaps you could say I had two life goals. The one from childhood being to catch a Megalodon, but the other came later in life. And now, I'll never attain either."

"What do you mean?" he asked. "What was the other one?"

He shook his head, but laughed sadly. "It was Katherine. When I took the bullet from her, I already loved her from afar. I'd seen her for the first time that very night, and was watching her. Trying to get up the nerve to speak to her. Oh, Will. She was a beautiful young woman." He met Will's eyes. "That's how I saw the gun. I was approaching her with some useless string of conversation planned to get her attention, and there the assassin was. It was instinct to save her, to take that bullet. I couldn't let anything happen to her.

"Now, all these years later, she's dead. It's my fault for bringing her here. I wanted her to be a part of it. I just wanted..." He trailed off.

"Wanted what?" Will urged.

He looked down again. "You remember saying your parents loved one another so very deeply?"

"Yeah, you asked me."

"I wanted that in my life. I wanted her to love me the way I did her, but she never did. She wouldn't say it, but I could tell. I felt it. There was so much pressure from society for us to pair and marry after the incident. The romantics playing games with royalty through gossip, as usual. Katty gave in, and I was all too happy that she did. Never said anything, but I knew." He leaned back into the crate and this time, unloaded the rocket launcher without effort and dropped it on deck.

"Will, take this to James and have him secure it to the deck. We can't lose it." His voice was emotionless. It seemed to Will that Sir Mallory, simply by uttering the words aloud, had gone as cold as the Antarctic after. His emotions froze up like the ice they'd been freed of earlier. Now, he faced his own survival being his meaning for living. Will suspected that for someone like Sir Mallory, that wouldn't be enough.

He hauled up the giant gun, tried to think of something to say to make Sir Mallory feel better, but decided it was better to leave him be.

After James had the missile launcher roped to the fire pit where anyone could operate it or free it from its slipknots, Ellen appeared on deck. To Will, she looked awful, with dark blue circles under her eyes and cheeks pale.

"Hey, Willie," she said. "God, it's disgusting out here. Does that smell ever go away?"

Will hadn't noticed it anymore, but she was right. The exploding Megalodon had left all kinds of rank odors in the pieces of it still on deck. Nobody had time to clean up anything, and Will had a feeling they never would. This ship, if it ever docked again, wouldn't take to the sea again. Seamen were a superstitious lot.

"You're covered in blood," she said, looking him over. Even her voice was strained. Will assumed that was from all the screaming the night before.

He felt his face. It was crusty. Looking down over his thick clothing, he saw splashes of brown and black among little frozen chunks of what was once living matter. Man or fish, he didn't know.

"You should change."

"I'm okay."

"It's not war paint. Go change your clothes and wash your face. Your hands, too."

"I'm wearing gloves."

She pointed at his gloved hands. He held them out and looked. They were almost completely black with blood, and stiff from the cold. How had he not noticed his mess? Why hadn't he realized he'd be covered in the mess like everyone else fighting last night?

"Oh," was all he said.

"Come on," she told him. "Come with me. I'll help. God knows we have to keep our minds off this, off everything." Her voice choked up with those last words.

As they made their way to below deck, Will looked around through the swirling snow, his breath white in front of him. So few people. So many had died. The ones who had washed overboard...had they simply drowned, froze, or were they eaten, unseen and unnoticed by the others? Their lives chewed up and swallowed like shark sushi without anyone to witness their final painful moments?

His father sailed fast as the storm settled more. The sun continued its path up the sky, and the pair went below to clean Will's demolished wardrobe and face of blood and guts.

CHAPTER 16

Will was tired, yet alert. Maybe just his body was tired, he reasoned, because his mind felt sharp as sin. No, he never would sleep again.

They'd been sailing for several hours. Tension filled the snowy air. It seemed colder, the seas rougher, but Will still hadn't gotten sick again. It was amazing, but not something he dwelled on. He wondered if all this time he'd spent too much energy focusing on being seasick and that was the root of it all. Now, there were other things to worry about, much bigger things.

Probably, though, it was the constant fear keeping him steady. Plus, he had to take care of Ellen. She wasn't doing well. They'd been on the bridge sitting in chairs, listening to their father and Don Mack navigate, run the ship. Every once in a while, Ellen would melodically mutter under her breath and Will would look over at her. Her eyes would be closed, head down, matted hair swaying crazily around her cheekbones as she rocked back and forth. He didn't know what she was doing, but figured she was dealing with what she'd seen last night through these shamanic chanting trances. He couldn't interrupt her or ask. That would be intrusive, she'd say, so he decided the best thing he could do for her was to stay by her side and simply be there.

Besides, for the time being, it was nice to be a warm body without responsibilities except to simply be a warm body.

"We should be in safer waters by night," Don Mack said as the sun neared the end of the day. The sky had gotten darker and the snow had picked up.

"Why's that?" Ellen asked.

"Shallower waters ahead," their father replied.

"Thank God." She sighed, and then leaned back in her chair and stared at the ceiling. "I can't wait for this to be over. This waiting. It's torture."

"Ellie, you're alright. We haven't seen anything of her since last night," said Don Mack.

She kept her head back and closed her hollow eyes.

Will looked out of the window beside him at the ocean rushing by. His dad really could sail. He saw they were heading due north, but his father masterfully seemed to predict where ice would be and avoided it while barely skimming off course. Will saw chunks of ice that could ground the ship cruise by as though guideposts on the path to ground and freedom from the Antarctic sea's horrors.

His breath fogged the window in the warm cabin. He kept doing it, fogging the window, letting it cover back up, then breathing on it again. Eventually, he drew a little frowning face with a big, round, filled-in circle for a nose in his window fog. It faded and he breathed on it again. The face came back, as angry and sad as ever. Faded. He breathed on it again. The face reappeared. Will looked through its nose-window to the sea and wondered how long it would be until night fell.

Then he saw it, right through the circular nose of his frowny-faced character. In the daylight, amidst the storming snow, the long, slender white fin looked even bigger than it had at night. How close was it? Impossible to tell…the sheer size!

Will's throat closed up. He tried to call out a warning, but not even air came out of his mouth. His lips worked, his hands braced either side of his fading fog face, and he kicked his legs, hoping someone would psychically know what he was trying to scream.

The Megalodon was back, and it was coming right for them.

After what felt like hours, but was really only a few seconds, his father took notice of Will's behavior, because he grabbed the microphone and called out over the ship, "All hands, prepare for battle! The shark is starboard side! Get ready, she's coming fast."

Will regained his abilities and shot out of the seat just as Ellen jumped out of hers. "No!" she squealed, staring out of the window.

"Ellen, stay here. Will, you too."

"I want to fight again!"

His father turned to him, looking down into his eyes with a pensive look. "You did well last night, but now's not the time. We're ready for her. You're safer here."

"We're not ready for it! Look at how few people there are left. If she rams us with all her strength like the other one did, we'll need every hand we have. I can help. I can fight," he argued.

"If she hits the ship that hard, it'll rip us to pieces."

Will put his hands in his hair. "All the more reason to be on deck, to get to the lifeboats, to at least end up in the water."

His dad scrutinized him, and then sighed deeply.

"Let the kid go, Captain. He's right," Don Mack chimed in.

"Alright. Alright. Stay with Mallory. Get weapons."

"Sir Mallory gave me three grenades."

"Good. Use them sparingly, and put them to the best use. Three isn't much." He gazed over Will's head at the oncoming fin. "Go."

Will ran out of the cabin, zipping up his parka and pulling the hood over his head, wrapping his bare hands in thick gloves.

The air was as frigid as ever, and after being in the warmth of the bridge for so long, the sleet and snow felt like bee stings all over the parts of his face that were exposed. He squinted his eyes against the elements as he ran down the stairs and onto the deck, scanning for Sir Mallory.

He spotted him starboard, bracing the rocket launcher against the rail, with James holding the back of it. It was still tied to the fire pit, but the ropes had been loosened, giving slack enough for it to reach this fighting position. Sir Mallory screamed out in the fading light at the fin. "Come on, you bitch! You slimy, fat spawn of a whore!"

The remaining crewmen had stopped ship work and had taken up handguns, the techie whose name Will still didn't know had one of the three machine guns, and the two green-suited men had the others.

The fin came on, but slowly, as though trying to intimidate them all with its sheer oncoming size in slow motion. Will had seen how massive its head was, how wide its mouth, teeth and bite were when it killed Lady Katherine. They all had.

That head and those gigantic teeth were coming right for them, intent on revenge for killing its babies. Will knew it.

The Megalodon had held back the night before, but now, it had no intention of such caution. It took its time, knowing it was twice the size of the ship and had them at its mercy, firepower be damned.

It was as though it knew they were almost out of fight, almost out of weapons that would even come close to touching it, if that. Sure, the little ones went down, but the mama didn't get to its size by having the same impulsiveness of attack that its offspring had had the night before, bringing them to their deaths. God knows how long it took the enormous prehistoric predator to get to this size, what it had survived to live long enough to be seventy feet.

"Come on!" Sir Mallory continued. He was mad with fury and rage, his once-pale face now red, his eyes wide and bursting out of their sockets as he stared down the imposing white fin leisurely coming their way.

"What's taking you so long?" he beckoned. "You lazy cunt!"

Will glanced back at James, who looked afraid. He pulled out a grenade, put his finger on the pin, and waited, remembering his father saying for him to use them wisely. His gloved hands shook around the grenade.

Its excruciatingly slow descent upon the ship began to pick up speed, and within a few tense moments, the fin was right upon them. Its head surfaced, showing two enormous black, soulless eyes examining its battlefield. Just as it reached the side of the ship, its mouth came out of the water. The head, oh God. It was even bigger close-up than it was from afar on the beach at the compound. It took up half the ship's side. Its open mouth let out a ghastly, reeking, and putrid scent as the teeth prepared for the now-familiar lunge they seemingly used like magic, coming right out of its mouth before it attacked.

Sir Mallory snapped just then, because Lady Katherine's head was still impaled on the tooth. Now, her face was barely recognizable, blue, bloated, with empty eye sockets. Her bottom jaw was completely gone.

Sir Mallory yanked the Megalodon tooth Will had once handled out of his pocket, and sliced the ropes holding the missile launcher. He then grabbed it up in his good arm and hand, and in a crazy and surprisingly daring move, jumped right inside the gigantic mouth bearing down on the deck.

All in a quick movement, he landed on his feet on its tongue, and then wedged the rocket launcher in the Megalodon's mouth, propping it open, screaming curses the whole time through the howling wind and whirling snow.

The Megalodon was stunned, and its approach stopped dead as it began swinging its head violently from side to side, trying to dislodge the object bracing its mouth open, keeping it from breathing. Will wondered briefly why it didn't submerge, but maybe it couldn't with the missile launcher stuck like that.

Sir Mallory held on to her front teeth with his good hand, and braced himself against the rocket launcher at his back. He reached up to the tooth holding his dead beloved wife's impaled head with his treasured Megalodon tooth in his left hand, and dug into the root of the tooth, blood pouring over his head, face, and shoulders. He truly looked like a madman then.

Still, the gargantuan shark swung its head side to side, making the water around the ship violent and tumultuous. The ship rocked hard in the now even rougher sea.

Sir Mallory made quick work with the sharp, polished tooth, and dug out the giant's tooth bearing what was left of Lady Katherine's head, and held it out, screaming victory curses at the roof of her bloody mouth. His face was entirely dark red and slick, and the only thing that made him recognizable as Sir Mallory was his eyes.

He looked, for once, like he might just have fulfilled a new life's desire: revenge.

"Shoot the rocket launcher, Mallory!" Will heard his dad call out over the speakers. Mallory either couldn't hear him or didn't care. He kept holding up the tooth and crying out to the storm and the ship and the gods themselves. Will saw streaks of his pale skin appear down his cheeks and realized the man was crying.

"Shoot it! You've got her!"

Just then, all at once, the missile launcher slipped as the Megalodon finally thought to shift its tongue. It slid to the side inside its mouth, landing to the left of its tongue and against its bottom teeth, lodged there loosely.

The shark took full advantage of its freedom, and wasted no time in closing its sharp, serrated teeth around Sir Mallory.

Will watched in horror as it began to chew up the man who had become one of the people who had influenced Will's life the most in such a short amount of time. He saw Sir Mallory's stomach rip open as it chewed, and his face went blank as his innards spilled out into its huge mouth. Strings of intestines hung from between its bottom teeth the next time it opened its mouth, and now both of Sir Mallory's legs were completely severed from his body. Still, he was alive, stunned, yet holding desperately to the tooth with Lady Katherine's head on it.

In one last bloody gush, it finished him off, swallowing hard, and then submerged. Its dorsal fin still towered above the ship, and the fin circled with intent all around the ship as though trying to find a weakness, a way to get them without taking any damage as the machine guns fired. Nobody had wanted to shoot while Sir Mallory was in her mouth.

There had been a moment of true hope when Sir Mallory had the chance to blow the top of her head open with the rocket launcher. Will's dad had seen it, and even tried to get through to the devastated and broken-spirited man, but his madness had gone too far.

Will swallowed hard as he glanced over the rail at the tooth with Lady Katherine's head still on it bobbing in the wild sea.

People ran from side to front to back to side of the boat, trying to keep up with its frantic and fast moves, firing the guns and missing. Bullets would run out soon, and then what would they have? The rocket launcher was gone.

Will kept ahold of his grenade, staying starboard through the whole thing, stunned by what he had just seen.

Then, it started testing the ship for weakness. It rammed the port side of the boat almost gently compared to the real damage it could do, almost as though testing the beast that was the ship itself like it was a giant predator, that the tasty snacks living on it were parasites it could pick off, but that they were of no consequence. Of course, that's what it would seem like to the huge shark.

The boat rocked to the side, and people fell and slid on the slick deck.

Will miraculously kept his balance by grabbing the handrail at the last minute before impact, and his dad righted the ship just in time for the Megalodon to slam into the front of the ship, with more force this time.

Will fell back, but kept his death grip on the rail. Once it had hit, the fighters recovered quickly and ran to portside where Will was stuck to his spot, following the monster's fin to where it intended to hit next.

The gunfire deafened Will momentarily. He closed his eyes and worried about Ellen for a brief moment, and then opened his eyes, seeing one of the guns take chunks out of the fin, and blood sprayed out, and then leaked down the length of it. Dark red against gleaming white in the storming snow.

A green-suited man aimed down as it approached, now furious with pain and coming fast. Will saw it tuck its head under through the water's surface as it came in for a hit, but the green-suited man fired directly into the top of its head a stream of bullets that had to do damage, yet still, it rammed the ship.

Hard.

They all fell back, and Will lost his grip on the grenade. It rolled away and over the side of the deck, into the water, forever useless to him.

"Damn it!" he muttered as he caught his breath, having landed in the center of the deck. Had the green-suited man done anything? If not, they truly were screwed. The machine guns in the hands of the green-suited men were their deadliest weapons. Will's confidence in his grenade abilities was low, and he wished he hadn't lost that precious one of three. How stupid of him. He should have been holding on tighter.

The Megalodon hit starboard again, not as hard, yet deeper in the water than its other hits. The ship lunged to the side.

Will's mind's eye kept seeing Sir Mallory's guts, his eyes, his tears streaking the blood covering his face.

He snapped. He couldn't take anymore.

Will got up and ran to the bridge. He fell again and again with the tilt of the boat and the slickness of the ice on deck, but he made it to the stairwell to the bridge. He climbed it in three leaps and barged onto the bridge.

Ellen was balled up in a corner, and Will's dad and Don Mack were yelling to each other to be heard over the gunfire. "Taking on water! Taking on water!"

Will grabbed his father, and spun his around from the controls to face him.

"Now's not the time, son." He tried to twist out of Will's grasp and get back to sailing the ship.

"Dad..." And then he threw up all over the side of his father's clothes.

"Will!" he exclaimed, whirling around to him.

"Dad, Dad. I saw Sir Mallory, I was right there. I saw...I saw...please, Dad, save us, you have to save us! I know you can. Please." Will's voice broke, and he ducked his head, wiping bile from his lips.

His father grabbed his face and put his forehead to Will's. "I'll get you and Ellen out of this. I swear to god. Do you still have your grenades?"

"Uh, two of them."

"Good. Good. Now—"

Just then, the Megalodon hit the port side with enormous force, and even Will heard the crushing metal of the hull breaching. Now the ship was taking on water on both sides.

"Dad, please," was all Will could say.

"I've got you, no matter what."

CHAPTER 17

Because the second hit was below water, the ship didn't fly across the sea. It was, however, enough to send Don Mack into a fit with the microphone. "Abandon ship! All hands, abandon ship!"

"Let's go," Will's dad said to him, and then grabbed Ellen up and to her feet. She seemed so panicked to Will, and she looked to their father with such despair that it hurt Will to see her like that.

"Get to the lifeboats, I repeat, get to the lifeboats," Don Mack continued, and then dropped the mic. "Let's go!"

They ran off the bridge as the ship tipped to portside, where the damage must've been terrible under the water's surface. The ship was, indeed, taking on a lot of water down below, and fast.

Will numbly ran with the others, worried about being on a lifeboat. How could they possibly survive on a lifeboat after what the Megalodon had done to the ship?

He slid and skidded all the way to the lifeboats, of which there were four. The two crewmen left were lowering on one as Will, his father, Don Mack and Ellen reached them.

A green-suited man could be heard firing a machine gun into the water, maybe in some desperate attempt at one last shot at killing her, albeit a stupid idea.

Maybe he wanted to go down with the ship. Wasn't that what his father was supposed to do? But then again, he promised Will that he would get them to safety. He had no choice but to trust in his father, that he could get them out of this like he said he could.

Will looked back at the wildly tilting deck as Ellen was ushered onto the lifeboat. James was trying to get to them, but kept slipping and falling on his side. At one point, he nearly slid off the deck and into the icy water, but hefted his lower half back up and continued on.

The Megalodon hadn't made another attack in all this time. Perhaps it was waiting to see what kind of damage it had done, if its last lunge was enough to exact its revenge.

Will was wrong.

Its head appeared beside the boat portside, black eyes rolling back as it opened its disgusting, gap-toothed mouth all the way, right by James.

James screamed when the smell hit him, fell down, and rolled onto his back.

The giant shark's teeth popped out toward the entire side of the deck, dead-center where James lay.

Crunch. As the teeth closed, James' body simply turned to a pulp of crushed meat and gushing, spraying blood. He didn't have time to scream again.

And Will didn't have time to register it, because the Megalodon had snapped the ship in half.

His father grabbed for his hand as he fell inward toward the collapsing ship, catching Will before he careened into the pit of metal folding inward.

He slung Will overboard, and Will sailed through the snow as though in slow motion, and at the last minute he had the sense to take a deep breath. Then, everything sped up and he hit the freezing, icy water of the Antarctic sea.

Will had never felt cold like this, and his lungs froze up, as did his limbs, upon sinking into the water. His senses were numbed, his brain on overload. He knew he needed to get to the surface, needed to get air and swim, swim far away from the enormous Megalodon, but he couldn't move. Not at all. He kept swirling in the mad sea, sinking…sinking…

His mother's face came into his mind's eye as he contemplated simply inhaling the salty water into his lungs. They burned for air. Will had only seen his mother in photographs, having been too young to remember her, but now, he saw her as though he were lying in a crib. Her long, brown braid swayed in his face and tickled his nose.

"What a good baby!" she cooed at him. "Do you know how much I love you?"

He smiled at her, gurgling, and took a deep breath…

An arm grabbed him under his armpits, wrapping around the front of him. He felt himself being pulled upward, out of the crib, and through the coldest waters he had ever known. Upon breaking the surface, he coughed and gasped, but still couldn't move.

"I got you," he heard his father say. "I got you, now grab ahold of me under my arms, stay on my back. Going to swim to a boat, come on. Move."

Will opened his eyes. When had it gotten so dark?

He knew then that the Megalodon had attacked because they'd been so close to being out of her swimming territory. Hadn't Don Mack said that by night, they'd be in safe waters? Too shallow for the gargantuan shark?

"Come on! We have to find Ellen." His father tread water in from of him, and spun around. "Grab hold."

Will made his arms move now that he wasn't anchored to his father's grasp. God, the pain from swimming in the frigid sea was torture. He tried kicking his feet to get closer to his dad, but nothing happened and he began to sink again. Just as his head went below the rough ocean's surface, his father pulled him up again.

"No time, come on. You can do it. You have to. For me, for Ellen."

Will grabbed ahold of his father's neck.

"No, under my arms, son. I can't swim like that."

With much pain, Will eased his frozen claws of hands under his father's arms and said in a tight, choked voice, "I'm on. I'm on, Dad. Let's find Ellen."

Last Will had seen of her, she and Don Mack were in a lifeboat trying to get her life jacket on just before he and his dad were about to climb aboard the small metal thing.

The Megalodon. It was still out there. Out here. Maybe it was right next to them, about to strike. Its rank odor hung on every air particle as though its open maw might be anywhere.

As Will's father swam, Will looked back over his shoulder. It took all his strength to do. The icy cold made all his joints and muscles stiff as though he were already dead, his body turning to the lifeless side while his brain still worked.

The ship was in two halves, both ends up in the air with the broken middle section sinking downward. He saw the Megalodon take another enormous bite out of the side of what was left of the wreckage, and the squealing, grinding sound made his ears almost bleed. It was worse than the sound of the missile launcher.

The Megalodon was so damn big.

He saw four figures in the water near the ship, and they swam away from the destruction. The shark hadn't realized that the snacks were getting away, and continued demolishing the ship in crunching, metallic-sounding, stabbing bites, but it didn't take the Megalodon long to realize the sacks of flesh weren't filling its mouth. It submerged, leaving only its damaged dorsal fin towering over them all. Had there been a sunset, its shadow would have passed over half the earth.

"Don't look," his father grunted to him between tight breaths of effort.

He wanted to look away, look forward to where they might be going, to where his dad was taking him to be safe. Ellen would be there, certainly. Of course, she would.

Still, Will couldn't stop watching the fin, the four men frantically swimming away from it in all directions.

The fin turned toward one figure. It had to be a green-suited man, because he lifted a handgun out of the water as the Megalodon's head surfaced, and those awful teeth opened for him. He shot into its open mouth, but it rushed at him, scooping him up, tossing its head back with him inside. Its mouth leaked blood down its white cheeks and its black eyes rolled back to white. The man's screams were not as loud as the ship's destruction, but much more painful to Will's ears. He just kept howling as though he never learned to speak, and he never would speak again. Then suddenly, as one of each of his arms and legs came out of the side of the monster's mouth, the screaming stopped dead. Like the man.

The Megalodon wasn't done. It went for the next figure in the water, who Will assumed was a crewman. He didn't have a gun. He turned to face the giant fish head-on when he smelled it coming for him, and ducked below the surface. The Megalodon was no stranger to being avoided at any cost, and diverted its attack by slipping its open mouth back under the sea. In the man's spot, the water burst in shades of crimson and black at the surface. His head bobbed to the surface, and Will was grateful for the darkened sky;

he couldn't make out the dead face's expression, but knew it was twisted in a mask of frozen horror.

The shark had gotten him below the surface, but brought its head out of the water to chew him up as though wanting the survivors to see her feed yet again, a warning that they all were next.

Will gripped his swimming father's underarms more tightly, but still couldn't look away.

The two men still in the water, the techie and a green-suited man, Will assumed, swam in their direction, but the Megalodon was onto them. Its fin swung around in the water, and sped toward their seemingly tiny, defenseless bodies.

It rose up out of the water, its nose skimming the surface of the freezing sea, and opened its enormous mouth behind them as they swam. Will couldn't see the eyes, but knew they were rolling back in anticipation of the double mouthful it was delighted to partake in.

The awful smell washed over him as he watched the Megalodon scoop up both men from the sea, but its aim was a little off—maybe from having to angle in two bodies at once. The giant teeth crunched both men clean in half at their waists as the shark lifted its head high in the air, and their innards and top halves of their bodies fell into the sea before the Megalodon. Its teeth made a quick meal of legs and feet, and then it finished off its small feast by first eating the green-suited man's upper body.

Next, Will saw that the techie was still half-alive and definitely aware as it swallowed him whole. His eyes were wide and terrified, consumed by fear and horror just as he went down the shark's gullet.

"Oh, oh..." Will murmured in stunned shock.

"Look away," his dad grunted. "We're almost to them."

To them? Will wrenched his frozen neck to look ahead, and away from the devastation behind them.

A lifeboat floated in the distance, and it held two human figures, but Will couldn't make out who they were.

Was one of them Ellen? It had to be. He wished for it more than anything.

"Almost there." His dad's voice was a mere husk from the effort of swimming in the icy sea with his six-foot-tall son on his back.

Will refused to look back again, and kept focused on the lifeboat, slowly coming closer and closer, and hoped…that was all he had.

They reached the lifeboat and Will heard Ellen's voice. "Dad! Will!" He felt strong hands pull his freezing, shivering body from the water and looked up. Don Mack hauled him onto the lifeboat as his father hefted himself aboard, as well.

Ellen grabbed him away from Don Mack and wrapped him in a tight, warm hug. She was dry; she hadn't gotten knocked into the sea. "You're okay, my God. I saw them…the others. I thought you and dad were out there. I didn't know who was swimming to us. We have to get away!"

As Ellen ran on hysterically, Will heard his dad thank Don Mack for saving Ellen. The first mate must have gotten the lifeboat to sea level just as the Megalodon collapsed the ship. Will hadn't seen it because he'd been watching the Megalodon's destruction.

"Oars?" Will's dad asked Don Mack.

"Right here, let's go."

The sailing duo grabbed up a pair of oars and started madly paddling south of the fin and the wreckage. Will watched behind them as the fin submerged, facing away from them.

Was it gone? Was it gone for good? Did it think there were no more snacks, that it had destroyed the threat and completed its revenge? He hoped so.

He turned forward and watched the darkening sea through the snowstorm, hoping they could get far enough away so that the giant shark wouldn't come looking for them.

He didn't know what would or could happen after that, but he didn't care. He'd rather starve and freeze to death on a lifeboat in the Antarctic sea than be eaten alive by the Megalodon.

A lump filled his throat and he continued to shiver as he wrapped a life jacket around him. It couldn't be this easy, but he hoped it was.

CHAPTER 18

How long had it been since the attack? How long had his father and Don Mack been paddling hard, trying to put as much distance between them and the giant shark as possible? It felt like seconds and hours and years all at the same time.

Will sat at the back of the lifeboat, shivering. Ellen had her arm around him, trying to keep him warm as the snowstorm died down. A single beam of the setting sun's light shone through the clouds on the horizon, lighting up the sea for a brief moment in yellows and blues and oranges.

Will saw nothing behind them, not even the fin.

His chest relaxed a little bit, and he took a deep breath. "I don't see it anymore. Dad, I think it's gone."

His father didn't acknowledge him, but rather kept pumping his oar in synch with Don Mack.

Ellen said, "Don't worry, Dad promised he'd get us out of this, and he always keeps his promises, Willie."

Yeah, he did, Will thought. Still, was this a promise anyone knew they could keep? Sure, his father was determined and had gotten them far, even seemingly completely away from the Megalodon. Had he tricked it? Were they really safe?

"Head for the ice, Don!" his father's rough voice called out.

Will turned away from where the havoc had been and looked ahead. A large chunk of ice floated in the now-disappearing ray of light. It was nearly as big as the Megalodon. Was his dad really going to get them on an iceberg? That was nuts! How could they be safe there?

How could they be safe on this tiny hunk of metal floating in the sea, either? Maybe his dad's plan wasn't that bad.

Will focused his mind on making the lifeboat go faster, as though through sheer willpower he could make this happen. His muscles were still stiff from the freezing water, but he wanted an oar, too. There simply wasn't another one. He considered dipping his wet, gloved hands into the sea and paddling, thinking maybe that little extra help might be all they needed.

In no time, they beached on the edge of the ice, and the two seamen pulled Will and his sister out of the boat and onto the slippery white surface. Ellen fell almost immediately, but Don Mack caught her before she went into the freezing water.

"Thank you, thank you," she said softly. Will barely heard her. She looked different to him now. Her eyes no longer held panic. She seemed downright pissed and fierce. She was now determined to stay alive at all costs.

"Here," he said to Ellen, reaching in his soaked parka pocket and pulling out a grenade, handing it to her.

She took it, stared at it in wonder. "I don't know how to use this."

"You pull this." He pointed at the grenade's pin. "And then you throw it at the shark if it comes back."

She looked up at him. "Thank you, Willie." She gave him a little smile.

"Come on," their father said. "We have to get as far into the middle of the ice as we can."

"But it's not coming back, right?" Ellen asked.

"Don't know, Ellie," said Don Mack, "but we have to be ready just in case."

"Have flares?" Will's dad asked Don Mack.

"Got them from the lifeboat." He held up a pack of three flares.

"Let's go." His father led the way, his black whip still hanging from his hip, swinging madly as he marched up and over the ice. The rest of them had a hard time keeping up with him. Will's father had experience walking on icebergs, even. Was his history still so much of a mystery to Will?

As they made it to the middle, highest point of the ice, Will's father turned to them and said, "We wait here. Someone had to have picked up one of our distress signals. We wait until we see something, and then we set off flares. Don't worry." He looked from Ellen to Will, and then back to Ellen. "I told you we'll be okay, and we will."

"I believe you, Dad," Ellen said to him.

His father turned to Will. "Do you?"

Will blinked hard at him and wiped a few snow flurries out of his eyelashes. The storm had almost completely died off. "Yeah, yeah, I do." He knew his dad had the best intentions of seeing them all to safety, but he also knew there was no guarantee, especially after all he'd seen.

"We should face away from each other, you know, so we can see every angle," Don Mack suggested.

"Good idea." Will's father's fingers grazed over the handle of his whip. "Will, you still have one grenade, right? And Ellen has the other?"

"Yeah." He took his out and held it out to his dad.

"No, you keep it. Don? Any weapons?"

"Just a Glock."

"If she comes back, hit her in the nose. That's her weakness."

"She can't get us way up here on the ice, can she?" Ellen asked, anger in her voice.

"I don't know," was all he said, and he twirled his fingers through the air in front of them. "Everyone, face away. Look out to sea. Alert us if you see anything. The shark, or a ship to rescue us, anything."

Will faced northeast, shivering. It almost felt like the threat was behind them. Even if the Megalodon came for them, it couldn't reach them through all the ice. Could it?

Time leaked by as the sky went black. The clouds parted again, and the snow stopped for the moment. Will looked up as the moon shone through the part in the clouds. It was a half-moon, one of the man in the moon's eyes watching their plight without emotion, but seemingly some knowledge of how all this would turn out.

He looked back at the moonlit surface of the sea. Lots of ice floated white among the waves' sparkles. It looked almost beautiful, if Will could forget why they were here and what might happen to them.

His breath plumed white in front of him as he kept watch, feeling bad that he'd even looked away for a moment to gaze at the half-moon. He could have missed something.

It was so quiet. No winds now, just a slight breeze. The water stayed rough around the iceberg, though, and the moonlight made the waves dance like mermaids were having a party just below the surface.

Will kept his sights on the black horizon, trying to keep his focus off the water and on the horizon. He kept his hopeful ears open for a ship's horn.

His breath was so thick with the frozen air that he couldn't see well in front of him each time he breathed out. He tried blowing down out of his mouth, but the breeze blew the white plumes back up in his eyes.

This went on forever, the waiting and watching. Nobody spoke. There was nothing to say; they were all thinking the same things. Would they be rescued? Would the Megalodon come back? Would they freeze to this spot, not having either of those scenarios? Their lives snuffed out quietly in a frozen slumber, bodies never to be found?

Will blew his breath to the side, white blowing away, and saw, in the light of the moonbeam, way in the distance, a long, thin, white fin rising out of the water, its tip blown to pieces and turning black.

This time, his voice didn't choke in his throat. "Dad!" He pointed, saying, "Dad!" again and again.

All of them turned and Ellen muttered a curse.

"I can't believe it," Don Mack said.

Will spun to his father. "Take my grenade."

"No, you need it." He rubbed his whip's handle again.

"Your whip can't do anything against this monster," Will told him. "Take it! I have no aim."

He shook his head. "You need it," he repeated.

The fin picked up speed, heading right for them.

"On your knees, everyone," his father barked.

They all fell to their knees instantly, preparing for impact. They were not disappointed.

The Megalodon rammed clean into the iceberg, sending them pitching forward onto their faces, then they rolled backward, scrambling to get back on their knees.

A huge chunk of the front of the ice had been broken off, leaving a gap of about thirty feet between the deadly sea and themselves.

The fin circled lazily in front of them, almost as though trying to decide how best to torment them for the shark's final act of murderous destruction.

"Don, your gun," his father hissed.

"Ready," Don Mack responded. Will glanced over at him. He had the Glock pointed in the direction of the shark. His father unclipped his whip and unwound it slowly, squinting one eye at the shark as some snow flurries blew in.

"Ellen, Will. Your grenades."

He held his up as Ellen wrapped a gloved finger around her grenade's pin.

"She's coming again," their father said, and Will looked out to sea.

This time, the putrid shark's smell oozed at them as it opened its mouth, coming straight for the ice. Its teeth gleamed as another moonbeam struggled with the heavy clouds. Will could make out the serrated edges of the front teeth still there, eying the gap where Sir Mallory had cut out Lady Katherine's tooth.

The Megalodon hit, its teeth biting down with as much force as it could on the ice in front of them. The impact wasn't as strong as a full-on ram, but the ice before them crumbled to pieces, and splashed in the water away from them. The iceberg shook, and Will fell to his side, his grenade almost slipping from his wet grip.

He sat up, dazed, to see that now, only about ten feet lie between them and the giant shark's massive bite. The fin danced in the moonlight, seemingly delighted that it was so close to more morsels of human flesh, so close to completing its revenge.

"Get ready!" Don Mack cried out as the fin straightened, and the Megalodon turned to face them again. With another bite, it could take them all out at once.

Its head rose out of the water as it came upon them a last time, intent on finishing this one way or another. Will saw the black eyes, this time not rolling back to white, and its teeth were so very sharp as its mouth opened, taking in sea water and expelling that disgusting scent. Will felt its warm breath on his face as the teeth popped out.

Suddenly, Will heard a loud explosion as Ellen hurled her grenade and it crashed into the top of the Megalodon's head. But it seemed to do no damage except to slow down the oncoming rush the giant shark made. Will couldn't see if the top of its head had holes in it or not, but the teeth went back in place.

He clung to his grenade, intent on not freezing up.

His dad cracked his whip upward as the shark's mouth closed in on them, and snapped it across the tip of its enormous white nose.

The shark stopped dead, closed its rank mouth, and submerged.

"Don, shoot her nose! I saw something. We can do this."

"I saw it, too," Don Mack called back to Will's father.

"What?" Will asked.

His father turned to him. "Get ready with that grenade, and try to throw it in her mouth when Don Mack shoots her nose."

The enormous Megalodon didn't stay under long, and its fin slung back around for another go, its head rising up out of the freezing sea, so close to them…so close.

Don Mack's gun let out a steady stream of bullet spray as its mouth opened, teeth shining, and Will closed his eyes and tossed his grenade.

He heard the explosion, opened his eyes. He'd landed it in her mouth! Blood came gushing out, and the shark was stunned by both the bullets to its nose and the grenade. It swung its head from side to side with its mouth wide open, and his dad ran up to the very edge of the rocking iceberg, held up his whip, and slashed it into the Megalodon's open mouth.

Will's shocked eyes saw the whip come out of the monster's mouth with something long, big and metallic, and his father guided the whip's bounty back to Will and the others. The missile launcher that Sir Mallory had left in the Megalodon's mouth had still been in there. That's what they'd seen. That's what his father and Don Mack wanted.

They might have a chance.

"Will!" Don Mack cried out. "Grab the front, now! She's coming again. I'm out of bullets. We got one shot at this! I'll hold the back."

Will skidded to the massive weapon and grabbed the front end, hunching to get the barrel over his shoulder like he'd seen the now-devoured techie do the night before. He felt Don Mack grab up the back as he watched the Megalodon, now absolutely furious, storm at them with a bloody, gaping mouth. Some more of its teeth were missing from the back of its gums—damage from the grenade explosion.

His father ran back to them as the shark's mouth enveloped the ice right where he had been standing.

"Do it!" Ellen screamed.

"Now!" his father yelled as the Megalodon's open mouth closed in on them and the teeth began popping out, and Will felt its putrid breath on his face again.

"Ready, kid?" Don Mack called out.

Will nodded hard, and with all the fight he could muster against the oncoming death, he aimed the rocket launcher at the Megalodon's mouth. It was mere yards away, and Will wondered why Don Mack hadn't fired yet. As the teeth crushed the ice in front of them, his dad cracked his whip one more time across the giant shark's white and bloodied nose, and then Don Mack fired the weapon.

Will swore he felt the missile move through his very body as it shot out of the launcher. He'd closed his eyes when he heard it, and now opened them in time to see the rocket shoot down the Megalodon's throat. Still, the beast came, the teeth closing down on them...and then, the explosion hit.

The Megalodon stopped dead in the water, feet from them, and Will heard its stomach rumbling like thunder. Its mouth opened and closed, and then a huge load of its insides came pouring out its mouth, all over them.

Human and fish body parts, muck and guts, and enormous amounts of blood poured over Will and the rest of them, covering their group and the ice around them. Everything turned blackish-red in the night. Then, Will couldn't see as blood and chunks of meat hit his face. He felt the Megalodon's warm blood soak through his freezing, wet parka and clothes. It was the first time he'd been warm in his entire life, he swore.

Before he could clear the mess off his face and out of his eyes, he heard Don Mack whooping, and Ellen cheering.

He felt a hand on his face. It was cleaning the blood out of his eyes. He was on his back. How did that happen? He looked up into his father's eyes and saw true, shining pride, excitement, love.

"You did it," he said.

Will found a smile for his father. "We did it. All of us."

"Yes, we did."

"It's dead?"

He smiled back. "She's gone for good."

He sat up and looked into the water, and the Megalodon's giant, white body was sinking in the frigid seas. It rolled around, and its fins and tail twitched wildly, but then, the whole huge mess of a prehistoric sea monster was enveloped by the water, never to be seen again.

"Wow," Will murmured.

"Wow is right!" Don Mack exclaimed.

Just then, from far off, Will heard the sweetest sound ever. It was the sound of a ship's horn.

EPILOGUE

"Come on, Willie. They have cool rocks in this shop." Ellen smiled up at him and tugged his arm, dragging him into the new age store at the corner of the Virginia coastal town's main street. They were visiting with their father, having taken time off from the ocean for a while.

Their father chuckled and followed them inside. Ellen immediately went to the case full of rock spheres of all sizes and colors. A clerk was there to assist her in pulling each one out almost immediately. She oooed and ahhhed over each one, saying she could feel this energy and that energy.

Will walked around, found a carved walking stick, and played around with it. Really, he was just waiting for Ellen to be done. He hated shopping, and disliked new age stores altogether.

"Can I help you with something?" said a smooth-sounding man's voice behind him.

He turned and saw a guy about his father's age bearing a long, gray ponytail and smiling.

"No, I'm alright. Just looking."

"Okay." He winked. "If you see anything, or are looking for something for your particular life needs, don't hesitate to ask."

"Okay, thanks," Will said, and walked away, feeling irritated. He wasn't looking where he was going, and had focused only on getting away from the hippie clerk.

He walked up to the far wall by a shop window where several wooden bins bearing trinkets was anchored to the wall. He looked down, trying to appear busy.

His heart stopped. He was staring straight down at a Megalodon tooth. Actually, about a dozen little, gray Megalodon

*

teeth. They were all around an inch long. They must've belonged to babies.

He instantly flashed back to when the rescue ship arrived on their little piece of floating ice in the Antarctic sea six months earlier. The Argentinians were stunned when they saw the bloody mess that was their island and them. They were questioned, but none of them told the real story. Will didn't know why, but he didn't feel like it at the time. He'd just wanted it all to be over. The others must have felt the same way, but all through the questions and the ship ride to the mainland, he'd noticed his father had a new light in his eyes, and at the time, he'd suspected it might not ever go out.

He reached in and took out the biggest tooth, which was about an inch and a half long. He ran his index finger up the serrated edge of the polished tooth, remembering Sir Mallory's giant one, recalling Sir Mallory's death, how he'd used his precious tooth as a weapon of revenge.

It got him killed in the end.

"Do those interest you?" Will heard the same man's voice from behind him. He turned.

"Those are Megalodon teeth, and the Megalodons were the apex predators of the seas around three million years ago. You seem drawn to them. I think I know why." He winked a blue eye again.

"Really?" Will said, unable to hide his sarcasm.

The man laughed. "Of course. You seek transformation. You see, carrying a Megalodon's tooth can bring about positive change in your life. It can reinforce old lessons and teach you how to handle new situations with a different perspective. It must be something you are seeking, because I watched you come right over here, straight to them. You seemed lost in a dream when you laid eyes on them. Yes, I think one of these are for you. Maybe even more than one." He smiled.

"Transformation, eh?" His father had come up next to them, having heard the conversation. "He's transformed a lot in the last, oh, six months. He turned thirteen and grew three inches."

"Thirteen!" the sales clerk said in surprise. He turned back to Will. "You look about seventeen. That is extraordinary. What a great time in your life for a shark's tooth. I promise, it would bring you through the painful transition of childhood into teen years with ease."

Will put the inch and a half-long tooth back in the bin with the others. "I'm doing alright, thanks."

The clerk tilted his head at Will's father. "He's so sure of himself for such a young age. You must be a very good father."

His dad looked at Will. "You'd have to ask him."

The clerk raised an eyebrow at Will. "I don't have to ask what you'll say. It's obvious that the two of you love each other very much. How lucky you are to have such a family bond."

Will glanced at his father. "I guess he's an alright dad." He smirked at him.

His father smirked back, and his eyes still hadn't lost that special light they'd found the night they obliterated a giant Megalodon together.

He turned back to the clerk. "I think I've transformed enough for now, but maybe later."

"Of course, of course," the clerk said, but he seemed uncertain by Will and his father's shared secret, sensing it, but not knowing with his all-seeing powers.

Ellen came up behind them as the clerk nodded and walked away, and she saw the Megalodon teeth. "Hmm." She picked one up, held it out. "These are kind of shitty and small, don't you think?"

"Watch your language," their father said without commitment.

"Learned it from you." She tossed the tooth back in the bin. "Let's get the hell out of here."

Will and his father grinned, and the three of them left. They were meeting Don Mack and his girlfriend for lunch a couple blocks away, and their father hated being late.

"Dad," Will said as they walked down the street, "Thanks."

He glanced at Will. "For what?"

He smiled up at his father. "For being a great dad."

Red crept up his father's cheeks, but it wasn't a blush of embarrassment, but rather feeling deep emotion bringing color to his weathered face.

"Thanks for being the best son I could hope for," he replied. "And Will?"

"Yeah?"

"I'm so glad you found your sea legs. Hurricane season is coming. Think you'd...?"

Will laughed. "Sure, why not? I think we can handle a little weather."

THE END

CHECK OUT OTHER GREAT DEEP SEA THRILLERS

MEGA
by Jake Bible

There is something in the deep. Something large. Something hungry. Something prehistoric.
And Team Grendel must find it, fight it, and kill it.
Kinsey Thorne, the first female US Navy SEAL candidate has hit rock bottom. Having washed out of the Navy, she turned to every drink and drug she could get her hands on. Until her father and cousins, all ex-Navy SEALS themselves, offer her a way back into the life: as part of a private, elite combat Team being put together to find and hunt down an impossible monster in the Indian Ocean. Kinsey has a second chance, but can she live through it?

THE BLACK
by Paul E Cooley

Under 30,000 feet of water, the exploration rig Leaguer has discovered an oil field larger than Saudi Arabia, with oil so sweet and pure, nations would go to war for the rights to it. But as the team starts drilling exploration well after exploration well in their race to claim the sweet crude, a deep rumbling beneath the ocean floor shakes them all to their core. Something has been living in the oil and it's about to give birth to the greatest threat humanity has ever seen.

"The Black" is a techno/horror-thriller that puts the horror and action of movies such as Leviathan and The Thing right into readers' hands. Ocean exploration will never be the same."

CHECK OUT OTHER GREAT
DEEP SEA THRILLERS

PREDATOR X
by C.J Waller

When deep level oil fracking uncovers a vast subterranean sea, a crack team of cavers and scientists are sent down to investigate. Upon their arrival, they disappear without a trace. A second team, including sedimentologist Dr Megan Stoker, are ordered to seek out Alpha Team and report back their findings. But Alpha team are nowhere to be found – instead, they are faced with something unexpected in the depths. Something ancient. Something huge. Something dangerous. Predator X

DEAD BAIT
by Tim Curran

A husband hell-bent on revenge hunts a Wereshark...A Russian mail order bride with a fishy secret...Crabs with a collective consciousness...A vampire who transforms into a Candiru...Zombie piranha...Bait that will have you crawling out of your skin and more. Drawing on horror, humor with a helping of dark fantasy and a touch of deviance, these 19 contemporary stories pay homage to the monsters that lurk in the murky waters of our imaginations. If you thought it was safe to go back in the water...Think Again!

CHECK OUT OTHER GREAT
DEEP SEA THRILLERS

LAMPREYS
by Alan Spencer

A secret government tactical team is sent to perform a clean sweep of a private research installation. Horrible atrocities lurk within the abandoned corridors. Mutated sea creatures with insane killing abilities are waiting to suck the blood and meat from their prey.

Unemployed college professor Conrad Garfield is forced to assist and is soon separated from the team. Alone and afraid, Conrad must use his wits to battle mutated lampreys, infected scientists and go head-to-head with the biggest monstrosity of all.

Can Conrad survive, or will the deadly monsters suck the very life from his body?

DEEP DEVOTION
by M.C. Norris

Rising from the depths, a mind-bending monster unleashes a wave of terror across the American heartland. Kate Browning, a Kansas City EMT confronts her paralyzing fear of water when she traces the source of a deadly parasitic affliction to the Gulf of Mexico. Cooperating with a marine biologist, she travels to Florida in an effort to save the life of one very special patient, but the source of the epidemic happens to be the nest of a terrifying monster, one that last rose from the depths to annihilate the lost continent of Atlantis.

Leviathan, destroyer, devoted lifemate and parent, the abomination is not going to take the extermination of its brood well.

CHECK OUT OTHER GREAT
DEEP SEA THRILLERS

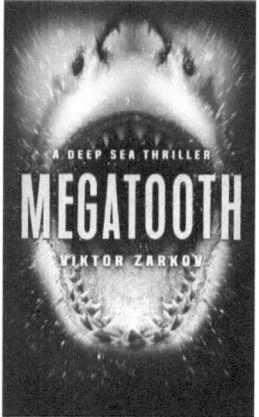

MEGATOOTH
by Viktor Zarkov

When the death rate of sperm whales rises dramatically, a well-respected environmental activist puts together a ragtag team to hit the high seas to investigate the matter. They suspect that the deaths are due to poachers and they are all driven by a need for justice.

Elsewhere, an experimental government vessel is enhancing deep sea mining equipment. They see one of these dead whales up close and personal...and are fairly certain that it wasn't poachers that killed it.

Both of these teams are about to discover that poachers are the least of their worries. There is something hunting the whales...

Something big
Something prehistoric.
Something terrifying.
MEGATOOTH!

BLOOD CRUISE
by Jake Bible

Ben Clow's plans are set. Drop off kids, pick up girlfriend, head to the marina, and hop on best friend's cruiser for a weekend of fun at sea. But Ben's happy plans are about to be changed by a tentacled horror that lurks beneath the waves.

International crime lords! Deep cover black ops agents! A ravenous, bloodsucking monster! A storm of evil and danger conspire to turn Ben Clow's vacation from a fun ocean getaway into a nightmare of a Blood Cruise!

www.ingramcontent.com/pod-product-compliance
Lightning Source LLC
Chambersburg PA
CBHW052002170626
46808CB00007B/2736